Jo was swept away on a wave of desire...

All the hunger of years poured into their kiss, with Jo giving and taking with breathless abandon. She clung to him, her hands moving restlessly over his shoulders, her fingers burying themselves in the rough thickness of his hair, pressing, wildly encouraging the expression of a love that was consuming her. Mike was molding her soft roundness to the hard length of his body with demanding pressure. It felt so right, so gloriously satisfying, and she willingly melted against him. When he finally dragged his mouth away from hers it was only to trail his lips down the curve of her throat. She shivered with delight, mesmerized by the sheer sensuality of his touch.

"Say you're mine, Jo," he breathed in her ear.

"Yes," she whispered huskily. "I love you, Mike."

EMMA DARCY

twisting shadows

Harlequin Books

TORONTO • NEW YORK • LONDON
AMSTERDAM • PARIS • SYDNEY • HAMBURG
STOCKHOLM • ATHENS • TOKYO • MILAN

Harlequin Presents first edition December 1983
ISBN 0-373-10648-3

Original hardcover edition published in 1983
by Mills & Boon Limited

CHAPTER ONE

OH God, it was him! Anguish sliced through Jo's heart, the shock of pain paralysing her. For one stunned moment she stared helplessly at him, but her recovery was swift. She lowered her lashes and urgently commanded herself to keep calm. He and his colleague were standing in readiness for introductions, but Jo could not move forward; she could not trust her legs yet. Bob Anderson brushed past her, his hand outstretched in greeting.

' 'Morning, Mr Hunter. I hope you're all ready for us here,' he rattled out cheerfully.

'Ready and waiting,' came the firm assurance as they shook hands.

Bob nodded towards her, frowning slightly at her immobility. 'Your programmer, Jo Standish.'

Still she could not move. Michael Hunter took the step she should have taken. He was offering his hand, but every nerve screamed to reject it. She disciplined the rampant emotion and forced her hand out. Strong fingers closed around it.

'I'm very pleased to welcome you to our staff, Miss Standish.'

'Thank you,' she heard herself say in a thin voice.

She could see the polite smile on his lips. With the utmost reluctance she raised her lashes. The gold flecks in her eyes burned with hatred, sharp pinpoints in green pools of ice. His facial muscles stiffened. The smile died, and incredulity darkened the blueness of his gaze. There was a sharp intake of breath.

'Mary.' The name was a soft sigh, barely a whisper from his lips.

'My name is Jo—Josephine Standish,' she clipped out with deadly emphasis. Her chin lifted proudly, defying him to contradict her.

He searched her rigid expression for one agonising moment and then nodded. 'Forgive me. I thought . . . we'd met before.'

Jo tightened her lips. He knew her all right. Something like dismay twisted across his face, then he was back under control. He turned aside, gesturing towards his colleague. Bob threw her a swift scrutiny, his eyes puzzled.

'May I introduce my cousin, Mark Hunter. He heads our Melbourne office and is vitally interested in our new computer operation. Bob Anderson, Jo Standish.'

Mark Hunter! Jo gritted her teeth as a surge of hatred forced bile up her throat. She swallowed it back down, determined to keep control. So at last she was to meet Mark Hunter! Her eyes focussed blisteringly on Michael Hunter's cousin as he shook hands with Bob. He was indeed tall, dark and handsome, every inch the copybook lover. Her sister had not stood a chance, Jo thought bitterly. He was turning towards her now, perfect white teeth flashing in a winning smile. She could barely conceal her distaste. Her skin crawled at the touch of his hand.

'It's indeed a pleasure, Miss Standish,' his voice crooned at her, oozing thickly with charm. His bedroom eyes suggested too much.

Jo snatched back her hand as a cold retort burst

from her lips. 'I'm not in the business of pleasure, Mr Hunter.'

The words were stinging with scarcely veiled sarcasm, rude in their impact. Bob goggled at her. His mouth hung open for one astonished second and then he rushed into speech.

'No, I swear Jo lives and breathes computers. They do her bidding without even a hiccup. Her progams always go through as smooth as silk.'

It was a deft attempt to rescue the situation, diverting attention away from her. Mark Hunter flicked an amused glance at him.

'Obviously a lady of considerable talent,' he drawled provocatively.

Bob's eyes snapped a warning as Jo took a sharp breath. Michael Hunter intervened.

'Shall we all sit down? There are a few points I'd like to get clear before you settle into your department.'

Tension permeated the air. Only Jo and Michael Hunter knew what was causing it, but Bob could smell it, and he did not like it. His eyes told her so as he took the central chair, effectively separating Jo from Mark Hunter. Cool it, he was flashing to her, this is a hell of a way to start a new job. But Jo was too incensed to give him a reassuring nod. Every atom of her body was in revolt against the situation.

She sat down and stared stonily ahead while Michael Hunter installed himself behind his executive desk. His eyes met her momentarily and the knowledge was there, memory sharply recalled and fully intact. Then an impassive mask settled over his face and he began speaking.

'You both understand that by the end of your

three months here, the new system must be operational. On top of that, my staff of systems analysts and programmers are to be fully conversant with the capabilities of the new computer. They must be fully trained to take over when you go.

'I expect to be informed of any hold-ups in the work schedule. If you find any member of my staff incompetent, I want to be told. They have been carefully screened, but you are the experts. You should be more discerning than anyone else. I cannot afford to keep someone in a postion where he can wreck the efficiency of the system. Any mistake there will be too expensive. From time to time I will call on you for reports, and I mean up-to-date reports. Now, do either of you have any questions?'

He paused, his glance sweeping them both. Bob raised an eyebrow at her and Jo shook her head.

'No questions,' Bob answered breezily, doing his best to project a sense of easy confidence.

'Good!' Michael Hunter turned his attention to his cousin. 'I think you'll find it profitable to listen in on this morning's conference, Mark. Anderson will be explaining the system to the men.'

'Good background to begin with,' he agreed readily.

Jo could feel Mark Hunter's eyes on her, but she disdained to look his way. She seethed at the thought of having to face him across a conference table. Michael Hunter's next words curled her stomach further.

'Mark is here to get a thorough grounding of the computer's capabilities for application in our Melbourne office. As he can only spare a fortnight, I would appreciate your co-operation in answering any questions he might put to you over that period of time.'

'Of course. We'll help in any way we can,' Bob jumped in, overflowing with co-operation.

Michael Hunter looked at Jo, the question still hanging. She met his gaze steadily, quelling the revulsion she felt. There was no necessity to answer; Bob's agreement covered her. The pause was mercifully brief. He continued speaking.

'Don't hesitate to contact me over any problems you meet. You're here to guarantee the success of the changeover and that takes priority over everything else. Now, I'll let you get started, Anderson. Mark, you go with him.'

The two men rose to their feet and Jo followed suit.

'Please stay, Miss Standish. There are a few extra points I wish to discuss with you.'

Her eyes challenged the order, but his expression was obdurate. She had no choice. She sat down again. Bob hesitated, clearly loath to leave her alone with Michael Hunter. His private antennae were still twitching at electric undercurrents.

'I'm afraid I need Jo to cover the programming for the staff, Mr Hunter. Although our work interlocks, she's the authority in her field,' he explained matter-of-factly. 'Perhaps you could wait . . .'

'It will take you some time to get the men organised around the conference table. I'll bring Miss Standish down presently.'

Bob was stumped and he knew it. Michael Hunter held the reins and he had just cracked the whip.

'Very well, I'll keep talking until she arrives,' Bob replied, toning down his demand but still letting it be known that he needed her. He threw her a wry look, an odd mixture of defeat and curiosity. He clearly did not like what he sensed in this room, but he was dying to know what was going on.

Jo was not deceived by the guise of business. Michael Hunter did not have computer programming on his mind; neither did she. The door closed and they were alone together. Yet not alone. The spectre of the past lay between them, imposing its presence more and more as the silence continued.

Jo forced herself to look at Michael Hunter with studied indifference. The brief business talk had given her enough time to recover from her initial shock. She was determined to keep her balance now. Hunt Surveys had contracted her services. She was here on business. The past was irrelevant, but its tentacles were winding around her heart, squeezing it relentlessly.

Those two nights of trauma and tragedy had left no mark on Michael Hunter, but then it was not his life which had been shattered. He looked exactly the same as she remembered him, handsome, hard and tough. His eyes were weighing her carefully, probing the smooth composure she wore as her first line of defence.

'Three years and three months,' he stated with slow deliberation.

'Give or take a few days,' she agreed, her tone one of dismissal.

'I didn't recognise you at first.'

Her eyes mocked him, knowing he was remembering a huge, graceless girl who bore little similarity to the slim elegance of today's model. Her height remained the same, all five feet ten inches of her, but the difference in appearance was like that between an ordinary family car and a Rolls-Royce.

'You haven't changed,' she stated coldly, a note of venom in her voice.

He leaned back in his chair and slowly reappraised her. Jo knew she looked good. The modelling school had taught her all the tricks of artifice, how to emphasise the tilted corners of her green eyes, how to play up the high cheekbones and play down the too-full lower lip. She no longer cringed to minimise her height. She wore fashionable high heels, sophisticated clothes, and her thick dark hair was looped down from its centre parting and then piled up high into a chignon above her crown. She had learnt that no one patronised a woman who stood proud and tall. And no one dismissed her at a glance, as Michael Hunter had once dismissed her.

'You could almost be a different woman,' he said thoughtfully. 'The question is . . . how different?'

'I'm surprised you recognised me at all. I can't imagine that I'm a person you'd like to remember,' she said with acid irony.

'Your eyes are the same.' He sighed, and one hand rubbed briefly at a slight scar on his forehead. His eyelids closed and he pinched them between finger and thumb before opening them again. 'God knows I've never forgotten those eyes,' he muttered. 'Why did you change your name?'

'I haven't changed my name. Why should I? There's no guilt or shame attached to it,' she flung back at him with pointed emphasis.

He sucked in his breath and the deep voice took on a gentler tone. 'I particularly listened for your name at the inquest. You gave it as Mary Standish.'

Her lips curled in derision. 'You seem to have a

habit of hearing only what you want to hear, Mr Hunter. I was asked to state my full name. Mary Josephine Standish. Mary, after my mother. I've always been called Jo.'

He hooded his eyes and leaned forward, absently picking up a pen from his desk and rolling it around in his hands. 'I shall make a point of listening more carefully to you in the future,' he stated flatly. Then he raised a keenly probing gaze to her. 'You knew this was my Company? That you'd be working for me?'

'Not until I walked into this office,' she answered bluntly. 'Hunt Surveys was the name on the contract.'

He paused, considering her intently. 'Would you have accepted the job if you'd known?'

Her chin lifted defiantly and proud green eyes issued a challenge. 'No man interferes with what I want to do, Mr Hunter. I go my own way. My private conviction is that you and your cousin should be consigned to hell, but I'm here on a job. This is business, and I keep business separate from my private life. You demanded the best computer programmer the Bureau could provide. I am the best and I'll do the job you're paying for.' There was no conceit in the claim. It was an honest self-appraisal.

'So this is purely business and you're prepared to work for me,' he said insistently.

'When I say I'll do something, it gets done. Can you say the same of yourself, Mr Hunter?' Her eyes condemned him contemptuously. 'You're the only person who has ever questioned my integrity. I wouldn't raise any question now if I were you. One unsubstantiated word out of place and I'll sue you for every cent you've got!'

'I don't doubt your integrity, Miss Standish,' he told her grimly. 'I'm painfully aware that I was a fool ever to doubt it. I deeply regret that mistake. I want you to know that.' He raised bleak eyes, fixing on hers with hard purpose. 'I tried to speak to you after the inquest, but you showed all too clearly that an apology from me was unacceptable.'

'An apology couldn't bring my sister back to life,' Jo interrupted bitterly.

'It was an accident,' he reminded her gently.

'Was it?' The harsh question carried its own accusation.

'You know it was.'

'In the eyes of the law it was an accident. You made a very good witness, Mr Hunter. All your evidence was tailored to the salient points.' She paused and then thrust home the deadly shaft. 'But you know and I know why Carol died that night.'

'Our interpretations might differ on that point,' he suggested quietly.

'I'm sure they do,' Jo agreed with heavy cynicism.

His lips twisted wryly. 'So you still believe that your sister was an innocent victim.'

'Carol was eighteen, Mr Hunter. How old was your cousin? Thirty?'

He looked at her with world-weary eyes. 'Age has little to do with willingness, Miss Standish, nor does it necessarily reflect innocence.'

'And you, of course, are quite the expert on judging innocence, aren't you, Mr Hunter?' she mocked him viciously.

It hurt him. He winced and then drew in a deep

breath. His eyes were still pained as he spoke. 'I misjudged you. For that I apologise.'

'How very magnanimous of you! Am I expected to be grateful that you've admitted a mistake?. It doesn't change the past, Mr Hunter, and I'm not here to re-hash the past. I'm here on business, and I might remind you that Bob Anderson is waiting for me to do my job.'

'He can wait! I've waited three years to speak to you and this time you'll listen. Your sister . . .'

'I will not listen! I heard enough rotten insinuations from you three years ago and I will not listen to any more on the subject of my sister!' Jo was on her feet, her eyes shooting sparks of contempt.

'Yes, by God, you will!' His fist crashed down on the desk as he stood up. 'I won't let you turn your back on me this time, Mary. We're going to clear this up now. Three years should have given you some sense of perspective.'

He had rounded the desk so that he was placed between Jo and the door and was now advancing on her with slow deliberation. Jo stood her ground, turning to him with icy disdain.

'My name is Jo—Miss Standish to you, Mr Hunter, and may I suggest that you get a sense of perspective. I don't work for you; I work for the Bureau. You've contracted my services, but there's nothing in that contract which requires me to listen to anything but business.' She drew in a deep breath and tilted her chin defiantly. 'Now, unless you have business to discuss, I'm going to walk out that door. If you lay one finger on me I'll report you. The only right you have is to demand the work you're paying for.'

He halted barely an arm's length from her. He was a big man, powerfully built, and the aggression emanating from him held her rigid, despite her defiant declaration. Then unbelievably he smiled. The blue eyes softened, caressing her warmly, and his face was lit with an immense charm.

'You haven't changed at all,' he murmured.

He took her hand and Jo was too confused to react negatively.

'Please forgive me for upsetting you. Come and sit over here and I'll order some coffee. I actually do have business to discuss with you.'

The sustained effort at control had weakened her. She allowed herself to be drawn over to where some armchairs were grouped around a coffee-table. She sank into one gratefully and tried to re-gather her strength. The high level of tension had drained her of energy. Michael Hunter ordered coffee over the intercom and she made no protest. It would be welcome. She closed her eyes for a moment. The morning, so far, had been quite harrowing on her nerves and there was more to come. Mark Hunter had still to be faced. At least he was ignorant of her identity, she consoled herself. He could not tap the memories which Michael Hunter shared.

'Cigarette?'

Her eyelashes fluttered up. He was pushing an opened onyx box towards her.

'I don't smoke.'

'Mind if I do?'

'No.'

He selected a cigarette and lit it, drawing on it intently. He sat across from her, his expression very controlled and thoughtful. Jo waited, outwardly composed but inwardly churning with a turmoil of emotion.

'You must have been with the Bureau for some years to have reached the top of your field,' he remarked.

'Three.'

'And before that?'

She looked at him guardedly. He was reaching back to that traumatic year when first her parents and then Carol had died, leaving her completely alone.

'I'm interested in your qualifications, Miss Standish. It could be helpful knowledge for selecting future programming staff,' he added in a matter-of-fact tone.

She relaxed. 'I was at university—I majored in Economics. I also did a course in Computer Studies. As far as selection of staff is concerned, you'll find that good programmers have certain characteristics. They invariably play chess or cards and enjoy doing puzzles.' She gave a little shrug. 'That may not be a steadfast rule, but it's true of my experience.'

'I'll keep it in mind,' he nodded. 'It must be quite an achievement to be considered the best when you're still so young.'

One beautifully arched eyebrow rose a fraction higher. 'Age doesn't necessarily reflect talent, Mr Hunter.'

His mouth twisted in wry appreciation of the parody of his earlier words about innocence. 'You don't think that experience counts for much?'

'Some experience is necessary, but you've either got the natural ability for programming or you haven't. It's more a knack of the mind than a learned skill.'

'What do you mean exactly?'

'You have to have an awareness of structure, the logical sequence which creates the end pattern. You can't ignore any step or the structure falls down. Computers have no imagination. They have to be told every detail and you have to be very precise.'

There was a knock on the door and Michael Hunter's secretary entered, wheeling a traymobile. She was a very shapely blonde who had no inhibitions about drawing attention to her shapeliness. Her tight skirt forced a mincing walk which emphasised the sway of well-rounded hips. She deftly transferred refreshments to the coffee-table and was completely unperturbed by the generous display of cleavage caused by leaning over. She finally straightened up with a toss of the shoulder-length hair and took a deep breath, inflating her prominent breasts further.

'Would you like me to pour, Mr Hunter?' she asked, her voice pitched with sexy huskiness.

'No, thank you, Suzie. We'll help ourselves.'

The impatient tone did not please Suzie. She departed, throwing a dagger-like glance at Jo on her way out. There was a distinct lack of innocence in the baby-blue eyes and Jo felt cynically amused by the suggestion of rivalry. If Michael Hunter's secretary reflected his taste in women, Jo was singularly unimpressed.

'Black or white?'

'White, please.'

He poured out the coffee and pushed cream and sugar towards her. The small mechanics of serving herself put Jo more at ease. Provided Michael Hunter kept to business she could field his questions without tension. It was the personal element which had shaken her.

'What you say about programmers is very interesting. As you know, our staff here are newly trained. From all reports they are reasonably competent, but I'd like to hear your personal opinion of them. Would Friday be too soon?'

'I should have a fair idea by then, but it wouldn't be conclusive. Naturally I'll be watching their work closely this week, but it may take them a little time to respond to my way of doing things.' She gave him a faintly derisive look. 'There's usually an element of male resistance to a female supervisor.'

'Is it much of a problem?'

'Only initially. They forget after a while.'

He grinned. 'A case of mind over matter.'

It surprised an answering smile from her. 'Something like that.'

There was a glint of satisfaction in his eyes which sent a warning tingle up Jo's spine. She sipped her coffee, savagely reminding herself of his identity. He would not worm another smile out of her.

'I'll be in Brisbane all next week. I'd like a report on their ability before I go even if it's not conclusive. You can give me your opinion over lunch on Friday.'

Jo bristled. 'Not over lunch, Mr Hunter. You're not entitled to my free time,' she retorted emphatically, her eyes coldly rejecting him.

He held her gaze, the blue eyes sharp and purposeful. 'You will lunch with me, Miss Standish, because it's the only time I can give you on Friday. I have a business conference in the morning and a string of appointments in the afternoon. You may have your free hour when I've finished with you. I do like to eat occasionally, and you'll fit in with me. Furthermore, I would be very surprised if the Bureau would take exception to that.'

An angry tide of colour scorched up Jo's neck. He had outmanoeuvred her, using her own taunt as a weapon. She had to accept.

'Very well. Lunch on Friday,' she agreed curtly.

'My secretary will call you about arrangements.'

She nodded and tried to swallow her resentment with the rest of her coffee. It did not work. 'Will I be obliged to lunch with your cousin as well?' she fired at him, hating the social implications of sharing a meal with either of the Hunter men.

He met her defiant stare for a long, tense moment before answering. 'That won't be necessary. Mark has enough time to fit into your schedule.' Then he added more softly, 'He's not the man you think he is, Miss Standish.'

She held his gaze steadily. 'He'll get my co-operation, Mr Hunter, as long as he keeps to computer business.'

'Fair enough,' he murmured. He drank his coffee and set the cup down. 'Your department is two floors down. If you're ready I'll accompany you there now and introduce you to the men.'

As Jo moved he stood and helped her up, then kept a guiding hand on her elbow as he led her out. Colour tinged her cheeks at the enforced proximity. She wanted to shy away, but dignity demanded compliance. It was a relief when the contact was removed. He paused at Suzie's desk to give a couple of instructions and Jo watched disdainfully as the girl fluttered her eyelashes at him. She could not deny that Michael Hunter had a strong sex appeal, but she knew better than to respond to it. He was not a man she would ever trust for anything.

The elevator ride down was short, and Jo was glad. Sharing a small, enclosed space with as big a man as Michael Hunter made her feel curiously claustrophobic. As they stepped out into her new place of work she glanced around with interest. The computer hardware was sealed behind glass at one end of the floor. The rest of the space seemed to be partitioned off into offices.

'Anderson would have told you it's an all-male staff on this floor,' Michael Hunter remarked casually.

'I don't mind working with men, Mr Hunter. I have no sexist prejudices.'

The terse little comment amused him. 'Elsie, the tea-lady, comes around every morning. No doubt she'll provide you with light relief.'

They reached an open area where Bob Anderson was holding forth to a group of men around a large conference table. His quick eyes noticed the faint curve lingering on Michael Hunter's lips and he looked at Jo with an air of relief. There was a stir of interest around the table as he gestured for Michael Hunter to speak.

Speculative eyes slid over Jo as she was introduced, but returned quickly to the authoritative figure who commanded their attention. He gave a brief address to the staff, stressing that expertise had been paid for and they should take every advantage of learning as much as possible while they could.

Then he handed the meeting back to Bob and departed.

There was a general relaxation around the table. Bob raised a quizzical eyebrow at Jo. She smiled and gave a dismissive shrug. As he proceeded to lay down the law according to Bob Anderson, she slowly settled her nerves. Bob's familiar drone had a soothing effect, and she looked at him with affection.

His sparse, sandy hair was already awry. The suit-coat was unbuttoned, revealing the bulge of his rotund body, and Jo made a private bet that his tie would soon be loosened. He was twenty years older than her, but they had a good working relationship. The gold-rimmed spectacles gave him an ineffectual, owl-like appearance, but he was the top systems analyst at the Bureau, with an incisive brain which could reduce any problems to workable equations. She had looked forward to this assignment with him. She would be enjoying it but for the Hunters.

Her gaze shifted to Mark Hunter, who was sitting to Bob's left. He suddenly glanced up and caught her gaze. A mischievous twinkle lit his eyes and incredibly he winked at her. She gave him an icy stare and pointedly shifted her attention to Bob. If Mark Hunter thought he could sweeten her up he was in for a sharp surprise!

Quite cynically she thought he should have found a career on stage or film. Those melting brown eyes, the dark, curly hair, even the trim moustache; all suggested a matinee idol, the leading love interest. No wonder her sister had been bowled over!

Bob wound up his spiel and signalled for Jo to take over. She rose to her feet, a surge of confidence overriding all other feelings. This was what she was good at. No one could take this from her, not the Hunters or anyone else. She sensed the male interest and reservation as she began speaking, but it soon dissipated under the weight of information she was imparting. Jo felt satisfied. She was at work.

CHAPTER TWO

For the next two hours Jo had no time to herself. Once the preliminary talks were over, Mark Hunter accompanied Bob to a separate office and Jo was busy with her team of programmers, handing out assignments and seeing they were understood. Her hope for some privacy during the lunch-hour was soon proved wrong. Bob Anderson descended on her, rolling his eyes in exasperation as he pressed her office door shut behind him.

'God almighty, Jo, what got into you this morning? And what the hell was going on up there?'

She shrugged off the questions with an apology. 'Sorry, Bob. I didn't perform very well, did I?'

'Perform! Perform!' His voice rose several decibels and he threw his hands up in a theatrical gesture. 'Oh, you performed all right, Jo. First of all you freeze into an iron maiden. Then you snap Mark Hunter's head off with a retort which curled the few hairs on my head. You sat up there as tensely coiled as a cobra and the electricity vibrating between you and Michael Hunter was positively explosive. To cap it all, I'm forced to leave you in private conference with God knows what about to blow up!'

He shook his head feelingly and slumped into the office chair. Having removed his spectacles and wiped them, he waved them around, jabbing the air for emphasis as he spoke. 'Let me tell you I was down here working my way towards a premature ulcer

while you were closeted upstairs. And then Hunter
turns up at our conference with a smile on his face!
Now, I ask you, what's a man to think?'

'You don't have to think anything. Everything's
fine,' she assured him nonchalantly. 'I know I was a
bit sharp with Mark Hunter. I'm sorry about that,
but I didn't like his manner.'

Bob covered his face with one hand. 'Didn't like
his manner,' he muttered incredulously and dragged
his hand down the fleshy cheeks. He considered her
for a moment and then hitched himself forward. 'Jo,
this isn't the Bureau. There's a little matter called
public relations where we try to get on with the
customers. Now you may not like Mark Hunter's
manner, but you grin and bear it. He's only here for a
fortnight. You can at least be civil to him.'

'All right, I'll be civil,' Jo agreed levelly.

He sighed and settled back into the chair. 'Well,
what is it with Michael Hunter?'

She carefully schooled her expression to reveal
nothing. 'There's no problem with Michael Hunter.'

Bob cocked his head to one side and eyed her
speculatively. 'He was right though, wasn't he? You
have met before. It's the only answer that fits. He
couldn't get us out of the office fast enough so he
could speak to you alone.'

Jo hesitated. Her private life was none of Bob's
business, but she did owe him an explanation. She
had inadvertently given him some bad moments this
morning and it was only sensible to clear the air.

'Yes, we've met before. It was a long time ago and
on a family matter. It's irrelevant to the job.'

He looked at her curiously. 'I thought you told me
you didn't have any family, Jo.'

Her voice sharpened. 'I don't now. I did then.'
The narrowing thoughtfulness of Bob's eyes told her
she had been too sharp. She gave a careless shrug
and projected indifference into her voice. 'As I said,
it was a long time ago.'

'But that's what he wanted to talk to you about,'
Bob persisted.

'Not entirely. He wants a report on his programming staff. Over lunch, on Friday,' she added, with
enough emphasis to put him off the track.

'Lunch, eh?' His quick mind pounced on the cue
and he nodded a couple of times before his lips
curved into a knowing little smile. 'A pleasant venue
for a business report.'

Jo's answering smile was ironic, her eyes gently
mocking. 'It's his only free time on Friday. He's a
very busy man.'

'Uh-huh.' Bob waved a hand in a carefree gesture.
'I wouldn't have the nerve to suggest anything else.
But do watch that tongue of yours, Jo, particularly
around Mark Hunter.' He heaved himself up and
ambled over to her desk, leaning on it as he spoke
firmly to her. 'It's only natural for a man to admire a
good-looking woman. Now, you make an art of
looking good, Jo, and you can't take offence at
attention you've deliberately set out to draw. Look in
the mirror some time, and be honest with yourself.'

'I dress to please myself,' she replied tersely.

He straightened up and shook his head at her. 'Jo,
I'm middle-aged and happily married, but that
doesn't stop me from looking at you with pleasure.
Be reasonable. You don't have to like the man, but
you don't have to cut him down either.'

'Oh, I take your point,' she assured him.

His face broke into a wry grin. 'You usually do—that's why I like working with you.' The grin widened and his eyes took on a teasing gleam. 'Apart from the pleasure of your company, of course. Though I know to my cost that you're not in the business of pleasure.'

The dry remark prompted an answering grin from Jo. 'It was a bit strong, wasn't it?'

He patted his bulge affectionately. 'I'm well cushioned against shock, but don't put me to the test again in a hurry—the old system might not take it. In fact I'd better go and soothe it with some lunch, not that I can rest easy.'

'I am sorry I worried you, Bob,' Jo said ruefully.

He gave an airy wave and headed for the door, opening it before pausing to look back at her, his eyes twinkling with amusement. 'Come to think of it, it makes a good story. My wife will love it!'

She laughed, but the laugh died on her lips as Bob disappeared. Civility to the Hunters was not going to be easy. Between them they had caused the death of her sister, and that could never be forgotten. Her mind drifted bitterly over this morning's conversation with Michael Hunter. His apology did not wipe away the pain, could not even begin to soothe the agonised memories.

Three years and three months. Time was supposed to be a great healer, yet it had only taken one second this morning to rip the scar tissue away, exposing wounds which still had the power to hurt and were pulsing with angry life even now as the years slipped away.

Jo had gone to Michael Hunter's apartment, believing it was Mark's, prepared to fight Carol's fight, but with no real expectations of a favourable outcome. She recalled the sickening churn of emotions as she had stood outside his door with her finger on the buzzer. She had not known who would answer her summons. Her only certainty had been that someone was living there and he ought to know Mark's present whereabouts.

Mark Hunter was supposed to have gone away on a business trip. Only his prolonged absence had depressed Carol to the point of revealing her pregnancy. She had begged Jo for help, desperate in her need to find the man she had loved so recklessly. Shock and panic had given way to compassion for her sister's distress, but Jo had come on this mission with a heavy heart. She despised the apparent amorality of the man she had to contact and was depressingly sure he would have no intention of marrying her sister.

The door had been wrenched open. A tall, powerfully built man had stood there, stunningly naked but for a towel slung around lean hips. His wet hair was all awry from a quick rub. His aggressive maleness had held Jo speechless.

'Well, what do you want?' he had asked irritably, his eyes having swept over her dismissively before making the challenge.

Jo found her tongue with some difficulty and croaked out, 'I want to talk to you.'

Impatience clipped his words. 'Look, if it's magazine subscriptions, forget it. You've already got me out of my shower and I'm in no mood for buying anything.'

The door began closing and instinctively she stretched out her hand to stop it. 'Wait! I want to talk to you about an urgent private matter. It'll only take five minutes.'

He hesitated, frowning at her. 'I don't know you, do I, Miss . . .?'

'Standish,' Jo supplied hurriedly. 'I have some important information for Mr Hunter and I believe this is his apartment.'

For a moment vivid blue eyes bored into hers, calmly measuring if she was genuine or not. 'I'm Hunter,' he answered curtly, a challenge implicit in his voice.

Jo was completely taken aback. 'M-Mark Hunter?' she stammered indistinctly.

He nodded.

She had not anticipated meeting Mark Hunter himself. She stared at him blankly, struggling to accept his identity, then blurted out the first thing that came into her head.

'You're back from your business trip.'

Again he frowned. 'I've been back for some time. Now what is this?'

Some time! Some time! The words bounced around her brain stirring up a fierce loyalty to her sister. If Mark Hunter had been back for some time then he had been deceiving Carol, pretending to be someone else when she had telephoned. Jo steeled her backbone and spoke in a flat, determined voice.

'We haven't met, Mr Hunter, but I've come about my sister Carol. May I come in for a few minutes?'

He gave a vexed sigh of surrender. 'I suppose you'd better. I can't keep standing like this, it's too damned cold.'

He stood aside and waved her in. Jo flushed painfully as she passed him, acutely aware of his

state of undress. Her confusion was increased by his
failure to show any recognition of Carol's name.
Either he was exceptionally forgetful or he was going
to play a hard game of poker.

'Please sit down, Miss Standish. I tell you frankly
that I have no idea what you're doing here, but I'll
give you a few minutes. I'm sure you'll excuse me
while I put on some clothes.'

This last was said with sardonic amusement at her
obvious embarrassment. Jo stared resentfully after
him as he disappeared down the hallway. He was so
sure of himself, so confident that nothing could
disturb him.

She could see why Carol had fallen for him. The
powerful physique, so casually flaunted, exuded
virility. He could have been chosen to model for
Michelangelo. The rough-handsome face was also
strongly masculine, the lines of experience emphasis-
ing its rugged attraction. He was at least thirty, Jo
thought in disgust. Those worldly blue eyes held
none of the uncertainty of youth. Her sister had been
way out of her league with this man.

She sighed dejectedly and looked around the spacious living-room. Everything reeked of wealth, from
the thick Berber carpet on the floor to the original oil
paintings on the wall. Jo recognised a Drysdale and a
Pro Hart, both vivid flashes of colour in an otherwise
neutral room. Whatever Mark Hunter did for a
living, he was obviously successful. Unless he had
been born into wealth. Jo glanced around again and
decided that was probably the case. Few men could
afford these possessions by the age of thirty if they
had started with nothing. The thought dimmed any
hope of a marriage between Carol and Mark Hunter.

A man from a wealthy background tended to choose a wife from his own class.

She was still standing nervously when Mark Hunter reappeared. Clothes seemed to exaggerate his sex appeal. The blue knitted shirt highlighted the colour of his eyes and the depth of his tan. Tight-fitting jeans hugged the slender hips and moulded the powerfully muscled thighs. Now that his hair was drying she could see it was dark brown with lighter streaks which could have been grey. It was thick and straight and fashionably cut. She wondered fleetingly what such a man had seen in Carol.

'I'm sorry, I should have taken your coat,' he observed politely.

'It doesn't matter. I'm not staying,' Jo said quickly, negating any move towards her.

He shrugged and perched on the armrest of a particularly large chair. 'You have my attention, Miss Standish.'

The uninterest in his voice roused Jo's indignation. 'I've come on behalf of my sister, Carol Standish. She's pregnant, Mr Hunter, and she's expecting you to marry her. I don't know what your intentions are, but I do think you should see Carol and talk about it.'

He regarded her in silence, his expression giving nothing away. Jo shivered. The man was subjecting her to a cold scrutiny that was undermining the little confidence she had. He stood up abruptly and reached for a packet of cigarettes from a nearby table. There was a slow deliberation about his act in lighting up, and when he turned back to her there was a steely look on his face that completely unnerved her.

'I don't know what game you think you're playing, young lady, but I do not know, nor ever have known, a woman by the name of Carol Standish.'

The stark denial stunned Jo for a moment. Then the blood rushed to her face as all the churned emotions of the night welded into a river of scorn.

'You liar!' she spat out scathingly. 'You unscrupulous liar! To coldbloodedly seduce an inexperienced eighteen-year-old girl is contemptible enough, but to deny any responsibility shows a rottenness beyond belief!'

'That's enough!' he cut in sharply, his expression menacing as he advanced on her.

'No, it's not enough!' Jo defied him recklessly. 'There's a great deal more, but I suppose I can't expect to reach a man of no conscience or morality.'

He gripped her shoulders and shook her, but Jo was too incensed to care.

'Do you get a kick out of acting the strong man, Mr Hunter? It's a pity you haven't a backbone to go with it, enough backbone to face my sister and say you don't know her!'

'Will you shut up and listen?' he grated out, his fingers tightening the grip, digging into her flesh.

The physical pressure had its effect. Jo's eyes focussed clearly, seeing the grim purpose on the face close to hers. The red haze of emotion disappeared and for an electric moment there was just a man there, a disturbingly attractive man who was holding her tightly, concentrating totally on her. A primitive yearning sparked into life and the shock of it brought her to her senses, her mind reeling under the shame of being affected in such a way. She shut her eyes tightly, denying the treacherous feeling. This was

Mark Hunter, Carol's lover, the man who had used her sister so shabbily and then ruthlessly cut her out of his life.

She took a long, shuddering breath and spoke as calmly as she could. 'Please take your hands off me, Mr Hunter. I want to go.'

'Oh no, you don't, Miss Standish. Not until we get a few things straightened out,' he said emphatically.

Before Jo could protest he forcibly steered her to a chair and pushed her into it. Then standing over her to block any move to escape, he arrogantly presumed to question her.

'Facts and figures, Miss Standish. Just when did this alleged affair take place? You've been making some pretty strong accusations, and you'd better be able to back them up.'

Something was wrong. It finally penetrated Jo's brain that this man was not acting in character, unless he was attempting a cynical bluff. Lifting her eyes to his and silently daring him to contradict her, she recited Carol's story with cold precision, naming days and dates and finishing with the prolonged business trip. It gave her some grim satisfaction to see his expression change. The challenge had obviously turned sour on him. A charged silence lay between them as he moved away and lit another cigarette.

'What is my name?'

Jo could see no purpose behind the words. 'I don't understand you.'

'Give my full name, Miss Standish,' he demanded.

'Mark Hunter, of course. What game are you playing at now?' she asked suspiciously.

He nodded as if in confirmation, then took the

chair opposite her, sinking into it wearily and stretching out his long legs. He eyed her thoughtfully as he dragged on his cigarette. Jo felt completely spent as she stared back. There was nothing more to say. She did not entertain any hope that his attitude could be changed. There was a ruthless quality about the man that defeated her.

'Miss Standish, I apologise for the rough handling. I'm afraid we both jumped to wrong conclusions. I didn't realise you thought I was Mark.'

Jo's mind whirled at the implications in his words. Her whole being churned with the necessity to deny it. 'I asked you if you were Mark Hunter and you nodded.' Her hands gestured around her. 'This is Mark Hunter's apartment.'

'I'm sorry, I misheard. This is my apartment,' he corrected gently, 'and my name is Mike—Michael Hunter.'

Jo shook her head. It was a trick. He just wanted to get rid of her, dispose of the problem. 'No,' she muttered stubbornly.

He was unperturbed. 'My identity can be easily proved. I can show you my passport if you like. Your sister should have added a description. Mark and I are nothing alike.'

She had to believe him. He was too calm, too confident. Besides, her mind was racing back over all his actions and words. They were consistent with ignorance of Carol.

'Who . . . are you?' she asked, casting her doubts aside. 'His brother?'

'No. We're first cousins.'

'Oh, my God!' she whispered, remembering the accusations she had hurled at this man, the blistering abuse. Colour scorched her cheeks and then slowly ebbed away, leaving a pale, stricken look on her face.

'Don't upset yourself on my account,' he said quietly. 'The mistake was mostly mine.'

'I said some dreadful things,' she murmured apologetically, her lips dry and tight.

'Forget it.'

'No. It was stupid of me. Carol said Mark was away. I was so tensed up about coming here that it threw me when you said your name was Hunter.'

'If you knew Mark was away, why did you come here, Miss Standish?'

'To get his address.' Jo struggled to get her mind back on the job. She was back at square one now. 'You see, we knew someone was living here—Carol had telephoned.'

'Ah yes,' he nodded. 'There were calls asking for Mark. I'm afraid I was rather curt. I don't run Mark's social life.'

'We have to contact him. Where is he, Mr Hunter?'

'In Melbourne. He lives there. Mark was only staying here while I was away on business.'

'Is he coming back soon?'

'Not as far as I know.'

The confirmation of her own suspicions only darkened an already bleak situation. Her eyes carried a mute protest as she muttered, 'Carol thinks he loves her.'

Michael Hunter stirred uncomfortably. 'I'm sorry. I doubt very much that Mark . . .' He hesitated and frowned. 'You say your sister's eighteen?'

'Yes, and desperately in love with him. Please, can

you give me Mark's address?'

He rubbed his forehead thoughtfully. 'I really think you'd be better advised to confide in your parents before tackling Mark with this. Your sister may not want to, but I think she'll need their support. I don't think marriage is at all likely.'

Jo knew he meant well, but she could not hold back the tears that glittered in her eyes. 'Our parents were killed in a plane crash six months ago.'

'I'm sorry,' he murmured sympathetically, and waited until Jo had regained her composure before adding, 'Is there any close family you can turn to?'

She shook her head. 'We only have each other. I'm sure if Mum and Dad had been alive this would never have happened. Carol's in such a state, Mr Hunter. She won't listen to me. We won't be able to work anything out until she's seen Mark. It's the only way. Please give me his address.'

He nodded but did not reply. His eyes narrowed and one blunt thumb rubbed at his lower lip.

'Mr Hunter?'

He raised one eyebrow questioningly.

'The address?' Jo persisted.

'I don't think that's a good idea. Forgive me, Miss Standish, but I think I'm in a better position to judge. Let me contact Mark. If his attitude is negative then your sister will be saved a lot of heartbreak and humiliation. I can reason with him and perhaps we'll be able to work something out. Give me twenty-four hours.'

The vision of Carol being callously rejected by Mark shattered Jo's resolve. 'She desperately wants to see him. I agree with you, but Carol won't. Do you think you can persuade him to see her?'

'Trust me to do what's best. I won't let you down. Where do you live?'

Jo believed him. There was a quiet integrity in his voice which soothed her troubled soul. She told him her address and he wrote it down, checking with her that he had it correctly. She sat there blankly, digesting the fact that he had taken the matter out of her hands. It did not register that he had moved until she heard his voice ordering a taxi. She stared at his back, grateful for his thoughtfulness and wishing they could have met in different circumstances.

'There should be a taxi for you in about ten minutes,' he informed her as he turned around. His eyes softened perceptibly. 'I would have preferred to take you home myself, but I think the time would be better occupied in trying to contact Mark. You look exhausted.'

Jo flushed painfully at such kindness. 'Thank you for everything. You've been so good . . . I was so rude.' The emotions which had been spent in this room seemed to crackle in the air. She stood up abruptly, anxious now to get back to Carol. 'I'll wait in the foyer.'

He hesitated, then seeing the strain in her eyes he nodded. 'If you prefer it. The taxi shouldn't be long. I'll go down with you.'

'There's no need. Truly, I'll be all right.'

'I don't want you to wait alone,' he insisted softly, stepping closer to her and placing gentle hands on her shoulders. 'You seem very young to be weighted down with responsibilities.'

'I'm twenty-one,' she stated matter-of-factly, struggling to combat the strange effect his physical closeness was having on her.

He smiled. 'Older than I thought. I'm sorry about the circumstances, but I'm glad we've met. You're quite a woman, Miss Standish.'

Jo frowned, unable to believe what her heart and mind were telling her. The message had to be wrong and yet it seemed so real, an instinctive reaching out to each other, a mental handclasp, a deep, inner recognition that this man . . . she shook her head.

'I must go. You're . . . I must go.'

'Yes, of course.' He slid an arm around her shoulders, keeping her comfortably at his side as he accompanied her down to the foyer. 'Will eight o'clock tomorrow night be all right?'

'Yes, thank you.' Jo did not pull away. His body was transmitting a warm reassurance. It felt good.

'Try not to worry. I can't promise anything from Mark, but I'll help you work something out tomorrow night, whatever happens.'

They stopped just inside the front entrance of the apartment building and Jo looked up at him wonderingly. 'You're very kind. I felt so alone.'

'I know.'

'How did you know?'

He brushed a finger against her cheek in an oddly tender gesture. 'Your eyes. You have remarkably expressive eyes.'

'Then I hope you can see how grateful I am,' she said shyly.

'That, and much more,' he said softly.

Again Jo felt caught up in a strange intimacy. The taxi blared its arrival with a peremptory tattoo on the horn. She tore her gaze away from his and they moved forward, Michael Hunter opening doors for her.

'Thanks again,' she mumbled as he saw her seated in the taxi.

'Till tomorrow night,' he nodded.

Jo rubbed at her forehead, trying to push the memories away. She had believed Michael Hunter. She had trusted him to carry out his word. In complete naïvety she had looked forward to his coming the next evening. She had wanted very much to see him again.

CHAPTER THREE

SHE would certainly be seeing Michael Hunter again
now, Jo thought bitterly. She had to spend three
months in his office building, programming his computer, training his men. The thought reminded her
that a full afternoon's work stretched ahead of her. A
glance at her watch showed there were only twenty
minutes left of the lunch-hour, and the hollowness in
her stomach demanded that she eat something.

Jo drew an apple and a fruit-knife from her briefcase. With exaggerated care she carved the peel
away in one long coil and quartered the apple. As she
sliced the quarters into bite-sized pieces and began
munching, she reflected that Michael Hunter had
done precisely that to her life, cut it into such little
pieces that the whole could never be the same again.

He had come the next night, at eight o'clock, just
as he had promised, but that had been the only
promise fulfilled. Jo had opened the door to him and
from that moment her life had started tilting askew.
Her memory fastened inexorably on that moment.

'Miss Standish,' he nodded, coldly formal, no
warmth at all in his expression.

The smile on her lips wavered and died. 'Please
come in, Mr Hunter,' she said more stiffly than she
meant to.

He stepped past her, his eyes sweeping around the
living-room before turning back to her. 'I under-

stood your sister would be here,' he remarked, and there was annoyed impatience in his voice.

Jo flushed at the implied criticism and silently cursed Carol's whim to take a bath at the last minute. 'She is. She won't be long. Please sit down, Mr Hunter.'

Standing, he seemed to dominate the room, forcing a shyness on her which she normally would not feel. He lowered himself into the nearest armchair, observing her with hard blue eyes as she perched nervously on the edge of the lounge. His aloof manner was puzzling.

'Did you get in touch with your cousin?' she asked, finding his silence too unsettling to let it continue.

'Yes.'

He bit out the word in such a peremptory fashion that Jo felt as though she had been smacked down. She stared at him uncertainly, not knowing what to make of his coldness. It was in complete contrast to the kind civility he had shown her last night. His expression was remote as if he had inwardly retreated from the situation.

'Do you mind if I smoke?' he asked abruptly.

'No, of course not,' she replied, moving quickly to supply him with an ash-tray. She resumed her seat, wishing fiercely that Carol would hurry. Something was badly wrong. Michael Hunter's attitude was not only unsympathetic, it suggested antagonism. He had lit his cigarette and was now regarding her with cynical eyes.

'I must congratulate you, Miss Standish. Not many people fool me so comprehensively. That was quite a performance you put on last night.'

Jo could feel the blood draining from her face. 'I

. . . I beg your pardon?' she stammered.

'Your sister knew what she was doing, sending you as her advocate. You were very convincing. In fact you acted so well I found it difficult to believe my own cousin. It was just your bad luck that I am one person Mark would not lie to.'

As fast as her colour had receded, it now returned in a hot, angry flush. 'Are you accusing me of lying, Mr Hunter?'

The contempt in his eyes was unmistakable. 'To put it succinctly, Miss Standish, the game is up. I'm here to close the book on it. Is your sister going to make an appearance or not?'

Before Jo could move Carol breezed into the living-room, the scent of bath-salts wafting in with her. She presented her usual pretty picture, charmingly natural, her skin glowing with healthy youth.

'I'm sorry for keeping you waiting, Mr Hunter. I'm Carol Standish,' she smiled, holding out her hand with blithe confidence.

He stood up and touched it briefly, a sardonic little smile playing around his lips.

'It's very good of you to give yourself the trouble of visiting us,' Carol continued sweetly, 'but it was really quite unnecessary—I only wanted Mark's address. Please sit down.'

Carol had dressed in a demure white blouse and pleated kilt. Her movements were consciously graceful as she settled into the chair next to him. She was obviously impressed by this very male visitor, and Jo winced as her sister fluttered her eyelashes at him.

'You see,' Carol said softly, 'I'm sure when Mark knows about the baby and we have some time to discuss the future, everything will work out fine.'

'I don't think so,' he interrupted curtly.

For the first time since she had entered the room, Carol darted a quick look at Jo. The frozen expression that met her eyes made her frown. Then she assumed a woebegone look.

'But, Mr Hunter, this is very important to me. I love Mark, and . . .'

'Mark doesn't love you, Miss Standish, and never pretended to, so please spare me the histrionics. I've already suffered through one charade with your sister,' he added with studied boredom.

Carol gasped and looked accusingly at Jo, but Jo was too stunned to react.

'Mark is the father of my baby,' Carol began again with less assurance.

'Do you have a medical report to support that statement?'

'A medical report?' Carol echoed indignantly.

'Come now, Miss Standish. It's easy enough these days to have an affair without being inconvenienced by unwanted pregnancies. Mark admits to the affair, but says he offered to take precautions. You assured him it wasn't necessary. How you became pregnant is therefore a mystery and I'd like to see some proof of the fact.'

Carol jumped to her feet, too agitated to remain seated. 'You doubt my word?'

'Is it so difficult to obtain proof?' he asked pointedly.

Carol whirled on Jo, tears swimming into her large, brown eyes. 'Tell him! You know I'm pregnant.'

'I've told him,' Jo said dully.

It angered him. 'Yes, your sister told me a very

poignant fairy-tale about an innocent young virgin who had been despoiled by my cousin. Now I'd like to get at the truth before we consider the financial angle. Mark is prepared to help with medical bills if there is a pregnancy. If and when a child is born, he will arrange to pay some maintenance through a solicitor. There will be no talk of marriage and no generous settlement.'

Carol dissolved into tears and sank on to the floor, leaning her head weakly against the cushion of her chair. 'How can you be so brutal?' she accused with a heartrending sob. 'I am having his baby—I am!' she cried pathetically.

Michael Hunter was unmoved. 'That's most unfortunate, if true.'

'Unfortunate!' Jo spat out, an inner rage cracking the frigid shell of detachment. Shock had made her watch this scene as if she had no part in it, but she was over the shock now and boiling with resentment.

He raised one eyebrow mockingly. 'Wouldn't you say it was unfortunate that your sister made such a choice? If she's pregnant it's by her own choice, Miss Standish,' he emphasised coldly. 'I hesitate to use the word blackmail, but it wouldn't be the first time a girl deliberately used pregnancy to squeeze a man, and Mark is reasonably wealthy. I understand your sister capitalised on his generosity throughout their brief affair.'

Jo opened her mouth, but was too choked with emotion to speak. What he was suggesting was despicable, nasty beyond belief. The contempt he was heaping on them was so totally undeserved, and she would not tolerate it any longer. Her sense of justice was outraged. To be so meanly judged and condemned by a man she had liked and respected was a crushing hurt. Pride demanded some redress. Her eyes glistened with unshed tears, but she would not cry—she would not! She glared her own contempt back at Michael Hunter.

'Is money all you can think of, you and your despicable cousin? You think everything, emotion and honour, can be reduced to money?'

'Usually,' he replied, stony-faced.

'What an indictment that is of yourself, Mr Hunter!' Jo said scathingly, her voice tightly restrained. She was determined to keep her own self-respect. Carol's behaviour was uncontrolled, undignified. It was shaming in the face of Michael Hunter's cold disdain. Spurred on by this shame, she recklessly disregarded whatever Carol might have wanted.

'We don't need your cousin's money, Mr Hunter. Our parents left us well provided for.'

His eyes swept around the room, one eyebrow lifting sceptically. The rented flat compared poorly with the luxury Jo had seen last night.

'We can get by without any conscience money,' she insisted hotly. 'Not that I think for one moment that your cousin has a conscience!'

'Rash words, Miss Standish. Do I understand that you're freeing Mark of any responsibility should your sister be pregnant?'

'Oh no, Mr Hunter. He will never be free of responsibility,' Jo replied acidly, 'but we'll make no financial claim on him. As unbelievable as it may sound to you, my sister loves your worthless cousin. She only wanted his address because she thought they could make a go of marriage.'

His eyes narrowed and a slight frown creased his

forehead. Satisfied that she had hit back at him, Jo stood up, drawing herself up to her full height. 'Now, if you've quite finished insulting both of us, I'll ask you to leave. I won't thank you for coming.'

'No!' The cry burst from Carol's lips as she looked wildly around. Tears streaked her cheeks and she fixed wide, pleading eyes on Michael Hunter. 'Please, this is between Mark and me.' She swallowed, her face working convulsively in an effort to gain control. 'I can get a doctor's certificate if he needs one. Maybe he's a bit upset right now. If you'd let me tell him about the baby it wouldn't be like this. You've been unfair, Mr Hunter. I have a right to see Mark, and you have no right to stop me!'

He hesitated, the lines of his face softening slightly before resetting in grim resolve. 'I'm sorry, but he doesn't want to see you, Miss Standish. He asked me not to give you his address, and I must abide by his decision.'

Carol threw herself back against the chair, her fists pummelling the cushion in a frenzy of passion. 'But I love him—I want him. Oh, Mark, Mark, Mark!' she sobbed uncontrollably.

If she had wanted to drive Michael Hunter away she could not have chosen a more effective course of action. He stood up, a grimace of distaste twisting his mouth. His hard gaze fixed on Jo, dismissing Carol's outburst.

'If you change your mind about the money, you know where I live. It's a permanent address. I won't hold you to your impulsive disclaimer.'

'Goodbye, Mr Hunter.'

The deliberate emphasis was not lost on him. He stared at her for a long moment as if searching for a truth which just escaped him. Then he nodded stiffly and let himself out the front door.

Carol was still slumped on the floor. Jo felt like collapsing too. The hollow ache in her heart begged to be eased by tears. But there was no one else to comfort Carol, and she had to try. She knelt down beside her and squeezed her shoulders in an affectionate hug.

'It's no use, Carol—he's gone. We'll make out all right. I'll look after you, don't worry . . .'

'No!' Carol heaved herself upwards, knocking Jo aside. 'I will get to Mark—I will! He must tell me,' she panted wildly as she rushed out the door.

'Carol, come back!' Jo called after her retreating figure, but the only answer was the slap of slippers racing down the stairs. Jo followed, anxious to stop her sister acting foolishly. She reached the front porch of the building just as Carol shouted across the street.

'Mr Hunter—wait!'

The front door of his car was open and he was about to step in. He glanced back over his shoulder and straightened again. The lights of an oncoming car picked him out quite clearly, a powerful man with a stern, uncompromising face. Carol darted out, blind to anything but her purpose in stopping him. Brakes screeched, vainly trying to bite on the wet road. Carol stood transfixed in the wavering headlights, spotlighted in the rain as the car skidded relentlessly towards her. The scream that tore through the night came from Jo's throat.

There was a sickening thud. Carol was lifted in the air and tossed like a rag doll against a parked truck. The car slewed across the road and smashed into another parked vehicle. Jo could not move. As if in slow motion her eyes followed Michael Hunter moving towards Carol's slumped body. He stooped and knelt on the wet road, his hand going out to touch her.

His body was shielding Carol from view and Jo beat at him as he resisted her frenzied efforts to remove him. Then slowly, almost reluctantly, he rose to his feet. Jo tried to push past him, take his place beside Carol, but he held her fast, preventing any such action.

'There's nothing you can do,' he said in a strange, hollow voice.

'No!' she panted. 'You don't know—you can't tell. Let me go, damn you! She's my sister!'

This last agonised cry broke his resolve. He released his grip and stepped aside. Jo had no time for him. She dropped on her knees, her eyes searching for injury. Carol's face looked deathly white and she was still, so horribly still. Jo picked up one limp hand and began rubbing it distractedly, fear slicing through her.

'How bad is it?' someone puffed, out of breath and anxious. 'I tried to stop—I tried not to hit her. My God, she just ran out in front of me!'

Michael Hunter's voice answered, calm and authoritative. 'It's serious. You'd better call the ambulance and the police. I'll stay here and look after them.'

'She's not dead, is she?' came the anguished question.

'I'm afraid so.'

Jo looked at the odd angle of Carol's head. She reached out to move it so that it looked right, but drew back, fearing it might be the wrong thing to do. She picked up the limp hand again and frantically searched for a pulse. There was no discernible beat. Again she reached forward, this time placing her hand over Carol's mouth and under her nose. There was no breath. Nothing. Her sister was dead—broken, finished. Like her mother and father. All gone, dead before their time—wrenched from life so unfairly. And Jo was alone—terribly, finally, alone.

The pain of loss sharpened and grew, needing an outlet because it was too much for her to bear. Her eyes focussed on the man towering over them.

'Why?' It was a grief-stricken cry of protest.

'I don't know,' he answered softly. 'It happened. There's nothing we can do.'

She shook her head helplessly. 'Why did you do it? For the sake of an address, a bit of communication, that's all.' Tears filled her eyes and joined the rain-drops on her cheeks. 'It wasn't much to ask,' she sobbed.

He squatted down so that their faces were more on a level. Carol's still body lay between them. Jo found a tissue in her pocket and tried to wipe the rain from Carol's face, impelled to do something for her sister.

'Didn't you know?' His voice was sharp, edged with strain.

'Know what?' Jo answered reflexively. The tissue was useless and Carol looked so uncared for. It wasn't right, almost indecent that she be lying there so exposed to the weather. A strong hand gripped hers, stopping the futile movements.

'Didn't you know what your sister was doing?'

Jo glanced up resentfully. 'She was running after

you. Let go of my hand! Can't you see she needs to be protected?'

'Look at me!'

It was a harsh command, snapping Jo out of her shocked daze. She looked.

'You didn't know.'

The appalled whisper was meaningless to Jo, but for one agonised moment they stared into each other's souls.

'I trusted you.'

The words stumbled off her tongue, questioning, accusing, damning. Sirens rent the air, wailing their message of urgency, sundering the tenuous line of communication. Jo stood as an ambulance turned into their street, knowing it was too late but welcoming it as a sign that something would now be done. A police car arrived behind it, and there was a subdued buzz of activity as the ambulance men got about their business.

'Broken neck,' one of them murmured. 'Must have died on impact.'

They set up a stretcher and carefully lifted Carol's body on to it. A sheet was placed over her. The stretcher was placed in the ambulance.

'Identification?' a policeman asked.

'She's my sister,' Jo answered tremulously.

There were more questions and she answered like an automaton, grief bursting inside her but sealed off from these officials. She was given the name of a hospital, and then Michael Hunter was interfering.

'Miss Standish is badly shocked. She's also soaking wet, as you can see. Her apartment is just across the street. Surely it would be more humane to continue your questions there, Sergeant.'

'Constable—Constable Harris. And you are—?'

'Michael Hunter. I was here when the accident occurred.'

'A friend of Miss Standish?'

'No, not a friend,' Jo cut in sharply, a sudden hatred breaking through the frozen horror. 'Just a stranger who had business with us, and the business is now concluded.'

The constable glanced from one to the other uncertainly before common decency overrode curiosity. 'I'll take you home, Miss Standish.' He called some instructions to his partner as he gently took her arm. She went willingly, gratefully, weary beyond measure.

Jo had not expected to see him again, ever. To find him here, to find herself actually working for him, was a savage twist of fate she had never envisaged. And Mark Hunter too. How could she be civil to them when they had so much to answer for? Yet she had to be. Her work demanded it. She sighed and slumped back in her chair, eyeing her desk dispiritedly. She would be working to make Michael Hunter's Company more successful. It was almost black comedy, only Jo was not laughing.

She thought back over this morning's confrontation. Michael Hunter's apology stuck in her throat, forcing an evaluation. Was it genuine? Did he really believe he had made a mistake about her three years ago, or was the apology a diplomatic move, a cynical attempt to blunt her hostility so that their working relationship could be manoeuvred on to an easier footing?

The more she thought about their meeting the

more puzzling it became. This morning she had been too consumed by her own feelings to consider Michael Hunter objectively, yet now she recalled that his manner had been cautious and considerate. For the most part he had fended off her attacks with gentleness, quietly determining her attitude and showing sensitivity to her feelings. It was only when she refused to listen to a repetition of Mark's lies about her sister that he had shown the hard ruthlessness she remembered so well. Even then he had backed off, gracefully accepting her ultimatum.

He had smiled that insidious smile and she had weakened. Damn him and his smile, Jo thought angrily. Neither could be trusted. He had not backed off from the luncheon appointment. Was he simply imposing his authority, or did he have some devious motive for insisting that she accept? The report on the programmers was not a critical one; it could have waited for a more convenient time. She did not understand him, but she knew one thing for certain: he could not be trusted.

She wondered if he would reveal her identity to his cousin. Mark would not guess it on his own. There had never been any similarity between the sisters, not in face, figure or personality. Carol had been average height, her curves more pronounced and topped with a stunningly pretty face, always vivacious, bubbling over with the enjoyment of life. The contrast between her and Jo made it doubly ironic that Mark Hunter should now show himself attracted to the more reserved sister. Reserved in so many ways, and a lot of them caused by the Hunters, she thought savagely.

A sudden burst of laughter drew her attention to

the fact that the programmers were settling back at their desks. The lunch-hour was over. She pushed all thoughts of the Hunter men aside and went into the adjoining office to get the afternoon schedule under way.

Although satisfied with the start made, Jo was relieved when five o'clock came. It had been an oppressive day with the unexpected strain on her nerves of first meeting the Hunters, and then suffering through the memories they evoked. She quickly tidied her desk. Without so much as a courtesy knock on her door, Mark Hunter stepped into her office, and Jo froze.

'My dear Miss Standish—' he began with a confident grin.

'I am not your dear Miss Standish!' Jo instantly cut back at him before Bob's warning could temper her reaction. She made an effort to control her voice and added, 'And I'd be obliged if you could knock before entering my office in future, Mr Hunter. I don't favour people bursting in on me unexpectedly."

'A thousand apologies,' he followed up blithely, completely undeterred by her cool reception. 'I've been closeted with your esteemed colleague all day and haven't had time to further our acquaintance.' He propped himself on the edge of her desk and regarded her complacently. 'I thought you might give me some background over a few pleasant drinks, then I wouldn't be so ignorant when we get together tomorrow. Don't you think that's a splendid idea?'

A gleam sharpened the gold flecks in Jo's eyes. Civility, Bob had insisted, and she would be silkily civil. 'I'm afraid I don't agree with you, Mr Hunter. Any explanation of my work can be done more efficiently in the office with all the paperwork handy. And, as I pointed out this morning, I never mix business with pleasure. I'll see you tomorrow, Mr Hunter, in the office.'

She rose to her feet, expecting him to take the hint and go, but instead his eyes ran over her provocatively, finally meeting hers with a twinkling challenge.

'You're completely and utterly correct. Business should never be mixed with pleasure. Will you give me the pleasure of your company over a few drinks? We could go on and dine somewhere if you'd care to.'

Jo slipped on her jacket and picked up her briefcase.

'I doubt that you'd find my company pleasurable, Mr Hunter, apart from which I have other plans. Good evening.' She nodded casually and walked past him out of the office.

'Not tonight, eh, Josephine?'

Or any night, you snake! Jo mentally tossed back at him, not pausing in her stride. He was obviously the type who expected any woman to be easy prey to his slick good looks and charm. At eighteen years of age, Carol would have been an easy victim. Mark Hunter had probably forgotten all about her, just one pretty face among many who had accommodated him over the years.

Late afternoon sunshine poured over the city, glinting yellow on smutty windows and sending long shadows across Martin Place. Fruit and flower barrows were doing a brisk trade with the homegoing crowd. On impulse Jo crossed the Square and bought a bunch of daisies. She needed cheering up and they would brighten her living-room. Armed with her flowers and a determination to put the Hunter men out of her mind, she headed for Wynyard Station and home.

CHAPTER FOUR

A LOW wolf-whistle heralded her arrival on the computer floor. It seemed that Jo was not the only one who was more relaxed on Tuesday morning.

Amusement twitched at her lips. She should have guessed! Barry Jensen was the office flirt. His smile was too practised. A gentle squash might need to be delivered some time in the near future.

Ian Cornish looked up from his desk and blinked at her from behind his horn-rimmed glasses. 'Good morning.' The words were stiff with embarrassment.

Jo flashed him a bright smile and returned his greeting as Neville McKay and Jack Barrington came strolling out of another elevator, arguing loudly about the merits of the cricketers chosen to tour England. They called out cheerful greetings and settled noisily at their desks. There was a certain amount of wisecracking amongst them before any work was commenced.

Jo smiled to herself as she organised her own office. The four programmers were an odd blend of personalities. Barry Jensen was brashly confident, Ian Cornish shy and cautious. Jack Barrington and Neville McKay lay between these two extremes. Both were quick-witted and very competitive, similar in nature, and yet Neville McKay was the natural leader.

It was going to be very interesting to see how they would develop as a team. As men . . . Jo mused for a while, then shook her head. They were interesting, but not really attractive to her personally. There was no man in her life at present, not since her last romantic attachment had dissolved into indifference about a month ago.

She sighed and opened up the folder she had laid on her desk. Somehow the four programmers all seemed rather callow compared to Michael Hunter. The thought jolted her out of her light reverie. That was no way to be thinking about Michael Hunter. He could not be attractive to her, not after all that had happened. There was no denying he was physically attractive, but that was just a shell, a fortunate arrangement of skin and bone. The man underneath had earned her rejection. One charming smile would not change her judgement.

She immersed herself in work, but it was not long before the first interruption of the day arrived. The rattle of the door caught her attention and she looked up to see a red, pudding face topped with wispy grey hair. This was quickly followed by a body of ample proportions set on short, stout legs.

'Found yer, then,' the apparition wheezed. 'I'm Elsie. Got me tea-trolley outside for yer to 'ave a cuppa. Told those fellers they'd 'ave to wait—ladies first, I always say.'

'Thank you,' Jo smiled.

'What'll yer 'ave, then? I missed yer yesterday. They said yer was with Mr Michael.'

'That's right. I'd like white coffee with one sugar, if I may. I'm Jo, by the way—Jo Standish.'

Elsie shook her head disapprovingly. 'Jo don't suit yer, pretty girl an' all. Not your fault, though. Some parents are daft with names. Do yer want bickies or cakes with yer coffee?'

'No, thanks. Shall I come and get it?' Jo asked, rising to her feet.

Elsie turned back to answer and stopped in her tracks. 'My Gawd! Yer must be almost as tall as Mr Michael!'

Jo burst out laughing at the comical look on the broad face. 'I can't help that, either.'

'No, I don't suppose you can,' Elsie admitted cheerfully. 'Still, yer carry it well, I'll say that for yer. Sit down, I'll bring the coffee in.'

Jo did as she was told. 'Not many offices have a tea-lady any more,' she commented appreciatively as Elsie served her.

'I like me job, an' Mr Michael wouldn't put me off for one of those coffeematic machines. I've been with 'im since 'e set up. 'E's a kind man, is Mr Michael —none better.' She nodded her head knowingly, then sighed. 'Well, I'd better go an' do for these men. I was gonna warn yer not to take any cheek, but I reckon they'll keep in line. See yer tomorrow.'

'Yes. Thank you,' Jo smiled, amused by Elsie's conspiratorial wink as she went out the door.

She understood now why Michael Hunter had spoken of the tea-lady as light relief. Elsie apparently held her boss in high esteem, but she had probably only ever seen his kindness, not his ruthlessness. It would be interesting to hear the tea-lady's opinion of Mark Hunter. She wondered if it would carry an equal respect.

The morning coffee break was just over when the subject of her cynical thoughts was ushered into her office by Bob Anderson.

'Jo, could you take time off to fill Mark in on your

core programs? Give him the lowdown on what's to
be stored in the computer memory.'

'Of course,' she smiled pleasantly, proving to Bob
how very civil she was. 'I have an hour and a half
before lunch, or if you'd prefer to leave it until this
afternoon . . .?'

'Mark?' Bob threw her a look of approval before
turning to his companion questioningly.

'Now will be fine.'

'Well, I'll leave you to it.'

He waved a cheery salute and was gone. Jo indicated a chair to Mark Hunter and prepared to get
down to business. 'I think it will be easier if you bring
that chair around this side of the desk and sit next to
me, Mr Hunter,' she began matter-of-factly.

'Mark,' he corrected with a smile. 'No point in
formalities when we're working so closely together,'
he added flirtatiously as he settled himself next to
her.

His manner was a clear indication that he was still
ignorant of her identity. Jo ignored his words and
went straight into an explanation of the programs
which were fundamental to the system. Mark Hunter listened intelligently, his questions always astute
and to the point. Despite her prejudice Jo had to
admit he had a first-class business brain. At times he
was even one jump ahead of her in understanding the
problems involved.

'Well, I think that covers everything,' she stated
finally, satisfied that he would not have to trouble
her again with his unwanted presence.

'Thank you. I've rarely been given such a lucid
explanation of anything.' The compliment was
accompanied by a warm, admiring smile.

'You're very quick on the uptake,' Jo shrugged. 'Bob must have given you an appreciation of the scope we plan to encompass.'

'Talking about appreciation, I'd like to show mine by taking you out to lunch. There must be some reward for a bout of concentrated effort,' he announced with a decidedly provocative note in his voice.

Jo stiffened, then firmly reminded herself not to be offensive. 'I'm paid a generous salary for any concentrated effort on my part, Mr Hunter. I find that an adequate reward,' she replied levelly.

'Mark, please. I thought we'd settled that stuffy nonsense. As for your salary, that's Mike's affair. I like to show my own gratitude,' he persisted, reaching out to halt her hands as she straightened the pile of papers on her desk. Having claimed her reluctant attention he asked again, 'Will you have lunch with me, please, Jo?'

She ostentatiously removed her hands from under his and faced him calmly. 'No, thank you.'

He frowned, obviously puzzled by the flat refusal. 'I noticed that your fingers were bare of rings, but I suppose it was too much to expect you were free of attachments.'

He wanted some excuse from her and Jo took satisfaction in offering none. 'On the contrary, I'm completely free and intend to stay that way.' She picked up her handbag and stood up. 'Please excuse me, I only have an hour for lunch and I don't want to waste it.'

He looked completely nonplussed as she threw him a bright smile on her way out of the office. Jo had to repress a giggle until she was safely hidden in the elevator, then she laughed outright. It was sweet to let Mark Hunter know that someone was immune to his charms. The thought of Carol's young vulnerability took away her amusement and brought a bitter resolve to cut him down as often as the opportunity allowed.

She mused cynically over the fact that her rejection had fired Mark Hunter's interest instead of quenching it. She wondered what it took for her message to sink in. Civility was definitely a hampering factor; it made the task of puncturing his ego a more subtle one. But she would do it—oh yes, she would do it. It would be her private little revenge for Carol.

On Wednesday morning she arrived at the office to find a posy of tiny rosebuds perched in a glass of water on her desk. Underneath was a card. Curious and unsuspecting, she moved the glass aside and picked up the note.

'I found a way to thank you after all. I hope this sweetens your working day. Mark.'

Jo dropped the card into the waste-paper bin. The posy of rosebuds was about to follow, but the sweet scent and the prettiness of the arrangement halted her action. It was not the fault of the flowers that Mark Hunter had bought them. She replaced them in the glass of water and settled down to work. After all, she reasoned, if Mark Hunter thought he could capitalise on his gift he was in for a sharp surprise!

Elsie remarked on the posy as she placed Jo's coffee on her desk. 'Ooh, rosebuds! Aren't they lovely? Someone tryin' to get on yer good side, eh, luv?' she asked with a pleased smirk.

A speculative gleam came into Jo's eyes. 'Is there

room for them on your tea-trolley, Elsie?'

'Now, why would yer be wantin' to give 'em away? Don't yer like 'im, eh?' came the arch reply.

'To tell the truth, Elsie, I didn't have the heart to throw them out, but if you'd like them, you'd be doing me a favour by taking them with you.'

'An' I suppose 'e might just see 'em on me trolley an' get the message,' Elsie chuckled, making several chins wobble alarmingly.

'He might,' Jo grinned. 'He's not very good at taking no for an answer.'

'A bit pushy, eh? Now don't tell me who. I'll keep me eye out for anyone who looks a bit peeved. You can tell me if I guessed right tomorrow.'

Elsie bore the posy out triumphantly, determined to spot the man in question. For her it was a titillating game. For Jo it was a deliberate hit at Mark Hunter's ego, letting him know how indifferently she regarded his gift. His response came on Thursday morning. He obviously forestalled Elsie because he appeared at Jo's door bearing two cups of coffee.

'May I come in?' he asked, but his eyes mocked any suggestion of refusal.

'Of course,' Jo replied casually. 'Is there some problem I can help you with?'

'Yes. You can share your morning coffee break with me. I'm in urgent need of female company, intelligent, beautiful female company,' he announced, placing the cups on her desk and relaxing into a chair. 'It seems I made the wrong choice yesterday,' he added with a rueful smile.

'I beg your pardon?'

'Rosebuds or violets. Perhaps you would have preferred violets.'

'Oh I see,' said Jo with an air of uninterest. 'I suppose you gave the violets to Bob Anderson.'

'Good God, no! What do you take me for?' he laughed.

'I don't take you for anything. I see no reason why you should single me out for flowers. I'm sure you've found Bob just as helpful.'

'But nowhere near as charming,' he answered glibly.

Jo reached out and drew one of the cups towards her. 'You have a strange idea of what's charming,' she remarked dryly, and took a sip of coffee. She firmly reminded herself that she must not give offence to an executive. Silence seemed the best course, and she ignored him, drinking her coffee in quiet sips.

'You know, you're a very intriguing lady, Jo Standish,' he declared abruptly.

Jo favoured him with a stony glance.

'You're turning the heads of every male in this department and you pretend to be completely unaware of it. I ask myself, is she unaware or does she have a superiority complex? Not that I think you shouldn't have a superiority complex. You are decidedly a superior woman. But I can't help wondering what makes you tick.'

'I'm here to do a job,' Jo stated unequivocally.

'Ah, but I'm here to learn my job, and you're distracting me from my purpose,' he retorted with a grin. 'A mighty powerful distraction, I might add.'

Jo raised one eyebrow sardonically. 'That's most unfortunate, but as it's completely unintentional on my part, it's not my fault. You'll have to wrestle with the problem.'

'I'd like to very much.'

Her eyes flared dangerously, but she controlled herself and withdrew into silence.

'What? No sense of humour, Jo?' He delivered the words as a challenge.

'You're wasting your time with me,' she stated flatly, finding the play of words too distasteful to continue.

'Why?'

'I'm not interested.'

'Perhaps I could interest you if you'd give me the chance.'

'No.'

He was puzzled, unable to accept her rejection. 'Do you think I'm married?'

'Are you?' she asked curiously, wondering if some girl had caught his fancy long enough for rings to be exchanged.

'Not now. My ex-wife and I were divorced a year ago. To all intents and purposes, I'm a free man. I see no profit in brooding on the past.'

'No, you wouldn't,' Jo said bitterly.

Her tone made him look warily at her. 'Have you been married yourself?'

'No.'

'An unhappy love affair?'

'That's a remarkably personal question!'

'I'm looking for answers.'

'Look for them within yourself,' Jo answered tersely. 'Now, if you don't mind, I have a lot of work on my desk.'

'It'll keep for a few minutes. I'd like to know what you mean by that.'

'I don't choose to let it keep, and I don't choose to explain myself.'

Faced with her air of determination, he gave in gracefully. 'I'll take your cup back. We'll continue this conversation another time.'

'Thank you,' Jo replied coldly, and turned her attention to the papers in front of her.

She dismissed Mark Hunter from her mind because she really did have a lot of work to do. Tomorrow she would be lunching with his cousin who expected to hear an assessment of the programming staff. Their efforts so far seemed competent enough, but she wanted to recheck thoroughly. It was important to Jo that Michael Hunter be impressed with her efficiency. He had meanly judged her once; she would make certain that he would never have grounds to do so again.

She spent the afternoon moving around the programmers, taking note of their progress. Several times Barry Jensen attempted to get too fresh with her and Jo became increasingly irritated with his immaturity. He was showing off in front of the others, and she decided to smack him down once and for all. The opportunity was not long in coming.

'Oh, Miss Standish,' he called out, 'could we discuss my entry point into your program again?'

The emphasis was deliberately provocative. Sniggers were being smothered as Jo straightened up from Ian Cornish's desk. Neville McKay had his hand over his face, but the smirk on Jack Barrington's was uncovered.

'You surprise me, Mr Jensen. I thought such an elementary point was within your grasp.' The words were coated with icy disdain. 'Perhaps Mr Barrington can help you out. Do you feel competent enough to take that on, Mr Barrington, or have I overestimated your intelligence too?'

The smirk widened into a sheepish grin. Before he could reply Jo's eyes swept around them all, demanding their attention.

'I don't expect any of you to waste my time. I value it and I'm sure Mr Hunter does too. It's costing him a great deal. I hope I've made myself clear?'

From Barry Jensen's rueful expression Jo knew that such incidents were at an end. There was plenty of time in the coming weeks to be more relaxed with the men, but the tone of acceptable behaviour had needed to be set. There was a subtle shift in the atmosphere as she continued evaluating their work. By the time she was finished the men were responding to her more as a person than a female.

Taking this into consideration, it was probably unwise of her on Friday to emphasise her femininity. The dress she had chosen to wear was almost sensuous in the way it clung to her curves. The cream silk was boldly patterned with autumn leaves, and only someone as tall as Jo could have worn it successfully. With her colouring it looked superb.

She stared at her reflection in the mirror and honesty told her that Bob was right about her today. She did want to draw attention. She wanted to see that telltale gleam of interest in Michael Hunter's eyes. Pride demanded it. Three years ago his eyes had dismissed her as not warranting courtesy, let alone attention. She wanted him to know she was no longer a girl he could bruise and wound. She had her polished armour on and he could not hurt her any more.

Her appearance evoked some cautious compliments from the staff as she arrived at work. Jo relaxed her usual reserve and smiled. They were really a pleasant group of men. They quickly sensed the ease in her manner and tested it with a couple of jokes. She laughed and was immediately drawn into conversation.

'I say, Miss Standish, do you happen to play Bridge?' Neville McKay asked eagerly.

'Yes, I do.'

'There you are, Ian—found you a partner! How about it, Miss Standish? We could have a couple of rubbers at lunchtime. Barry doesn't play and Jack and I are practising for a competition.'

'I can't today. Will Monday do?'

'Great!' he said with all the enthusiasm of an addict. 'We'll all bring our lunch so we can get straight into it. How's that?'

'Great!' Jo echoed with a grin.

It seemed that suddenly she was one of the boys, and there was no protest when she insisted it was time to work. The telephone in her office was ringing and she hurried to answer it.

'Jo Standish.'

'Susan Trigg speaking, Mr Hunter's secretary. You have an appointment to meet Mr Hunter in his office at twelve noon, Miss Standish.'

Jo was amused by the waspish tone of voice. It was perfectly clear that Susan Trigg had taken a strong dislike to her, and she had no cause at all if she only knew it. 'Thank you, Miss Trigg,' Jo said sweetly, and put the telephone down.

She attempted to get to work, but her concentration was oddly astray. Little progress had been achieved by the time the tea-trolley came clinking along. Elsie almost burst into Jo's office, puffed up with all the glee of gossip.

'I should've known it'd be Mr Mark with them flowers! E's very flash with the ladies and yer quite right to watch 'im, Miss Jo.'

She put down the coffee so she could express herself without restraint. Jo smiled encouragement, curious to hear Elsie's opinion.

'It was 'im that 'ired Suzie Trigg when Mr Michael was away.' She sniffed disapprovingly. 'Miss 'igh-and-mighty up there—doesn't like me takin' in Mr Michael's coffee when e's not busy with visitors an' such. Thinks she'll catch Mr Michael's eye—as if 'e couldn't do better than that! Huh!' Elsie's snort of scorn made her pause for breath and Jo was able to get a word in.

'I take it that Mr Michael isn't married?'

Elsie sighed as if it was one of the world's great disasters. 'No, 'e's not, more's the pity. 'E works too 'ard, I keep tellin' 'im, but 'e just laughs at me. I'll marry when I find the right girl, 'e says, but I reckon 'e'll drop dead of an 'eart attack first.' Jo's appearance suddenly caught her attention. 'Well now, don't that dress look nice. I wish it was Mr Michael's eye on yer instead of Mr Mark's.'

'No thank you,' Jo said emphatically.

'Now, don't yer be wipin' off Mr Michael. 'E an' 'is cousin are as different as chalk an' cheese,' Elsie declared knowingly. 'Yer 'aven't been 'ere long enough. I know what I'm talkin' about.'

Having delivered this as a parting shot, Elsie made her exit before Jo could make any reply. There was nothing she could say anyhow. Elsie saw Michael Hunter through rose-coloured spectacles; Jo saw him in an entirely different light. And she would be seeing him again in another two hours. She tried to get her mind back on to work, but somehow it was impossible to keep her eyes from occasionally checking the time. As the clock crept towards noon she was conscious of growing tension. With ten minutes still to go the telephone rang again.

'Miss Standish?' Susan Trigg's artificially husky voice was instantly recognisable.

'Yes, Miss Trigg.'

'I have a message for you from Mr Hunter. He's been detained at a business conference. He regrets that he'll be unable to keep his appointment with you and sends his apologies.'

All the words were polite and efficient, but they conveyed a malicious smugness. Susan Trigg was certainly pleased that Jo's lunch with Michael Hunter was off. Jo thanked her briskly and hung up. Her nerves had been so keyed up that she now felt curiously numb. She sat quite still, waiting for relief to flood through her veins. Instead there was a sense of anti-climax, almost disappointment. Her report was prepared; she had prepared herself to give it. Now there was nothing.

'How about accepting me as a stand-in?'

Jo glanced up to see Mark Hunter leaning casually against the door-jamb.

'I beg your pardon?' she snapped, angry at his unexpected intrusion.

He pushed himself upright and sauntered into her office. 'I was upstairs when Mike's message came through, so I thought the decent thing to do was offer myself as a substitute. No point in wasting a perfectly good table at Danielle's. They serve marvellous seafood crêpes.'

'In that case please don't let me detain you. Since I'm not now required to give Mr Hunter a report, I think I'll take in the lunchtime concert at Martin Place. Much more relaxing than talking business,' Jo added sweetly while getting ready to go.

'What a splendid idea! We can drink in the fresh air and sunshine with music as food for our souls.'

The blithe words made Jo pause as she passed him, her gaze fixing on him coldly. 'I wasn't suggesting that you join me.'

'It's a free world. I think I'll tag along anyway—it might prove an enlightening hour.'

'Or an extremely dull one,' she said scornfully, not bothering to hide her dislike.

She walked on, ignoring him as he fell into step beside her. He operated the elevator buttons, held doors open and generally assumed the role of escort. He chattered on inconsequentially, pretending she was accepting his companionship, even playfully answering his own questions as her silence persisted. When Jo entered a snack-bar to buy sandwiches he was right behind her, ordering more and handing over money for both of them.

'I'll pay for my own,' she hissed at him.

'Now, Jo, you wouldn't want to harass the shop assistant, would you?' he admonished her cheerfully. 'Much easier for him to give one lot of change.'

The man behind the counter was operating the cash-till. Rather than make a scene Jo capitulated, but she snatched her packet of sandwiches from Mark and handed him a dollar. A brisk walk took her to a leafy corner in Martin Place and she settled on a bench seat. Mark Hunter politely asked the bearded youth next to her to move along, and to Jo's chagrin he moved.

A Country and Western band was churning out an insipid ballad. It was not really Jo's taste in music, but she felt forced to give it her rapt attention. Mark Hunter munched his sandwiches beside her, apparently unaffected by her hostility.

'Do you like Country and Western?' he asked good-naturedly.

She ignored him.

He sighed. 'You're not very communicative, are you?'

'Why should I be?' Jo demanded resentfully. 'I didn't invite you along. You've pressed your company on me.'

'You interest me. I've never met a woman who was so self-contained.'

'Then I'm glad I'm providing a new experience for you,' she answered tartly.

'Do you live alone?'

'Yes.'

'What about friends and family?' he asked curiously.

'I have no family.' Again she remembered Carol and her words were edged with bitterness as she asked, 'What about you? Did your wife give you children?'

'No.' He gave a harsh little laugh. 'Children wouldn't have fitted into my ex-wife's scheme of things.'

'Did you want any?'

'Yes. At least, I did at first—in the first flush of happiness, you know,' he added cynically. 'But my wife didn't want to spoil her figure. Her very beautiful body won her a richer meal ticket, and she departed for greener pastures. He was fifty, short and paunchy, but many times a millionaire.'

So Mark's shallow attractions had not been able to keep his wife contented. 'Good looks aren't everything,' Jo remarked pointedly.

'Ah, but I'm a sucker for beauty,' he sighed melodramatically, misreading her comment. 'Look at you! Here I am, worshipping at your feet, and you step all over me. Why don't you have some pity and put me out of my misery?'

'I don't happen to have a gun on me at the moment.'

Her tart reply first startled and then amused him. 'Just as well,' he laughed. 'I think you might be too fast on the draw for my safety. Seriously, though, why not let your hair down and come with me to a party tomorrow night? I can promise you'll enjoy yourself.'

'I'm not a party girl.'

'Hey! It's a perfectly respectable party. Nothing you could possibly object to. Pleasant people, good music, terrific food. It'll be a fun night, honestly. Why not give it a try?' he said persuasively.

Jo caught back the negative response that trembled on the tip of her tongue, then a calculating gleam came into her eye as she measured the eagerness in his. He was keen all right, keen enough to persist in the face of open hostility. His treatment of Carol called out for vengeance. She could crush that king-size ego of his if she played the right cards.

'Well, how about it?' he urged.

'You want to try, is that it?' she said slowly.

'Maybe you won't find me so bad,' he grinned.

Her eyes mocked him. 'All right, if that's what you want.'

'I'll make sure you won't regret it,' he said triumphantly.

Your triumph will be very short lived, Jo promised him silently. Arrangements were quickly settled and she cut the lunch-hour short. She had had enough of Mark Hunter. Let him anticipate his pleasures, she thought sourly, knowing there would be no real pleasure for her in the party tomorrow night. She was only going for one purpose, and that was to exact revenge.

They parted in the lobby of the office building. Jo rode the elevator up to her floor alone. She stepped out and came face to face with Michael Hunter, a coldly angry Michael Hunter.

CHAPTER FIVE

'Well met, Miss Standish,' he said cuttingly. 'It might have been more polite of you to wait for me.'

'I . . . I beg your pardon,' Jo stammered, composure completely lost.

'I presume you received my message.'

She frowned in bewilderment. 'Your secretary phoned me that you'd been delayed and wouldn't be able to keep the appointment.'

'Delayed, yes, but our appointment was postponed, not cancelled. You have now wasted ten minutes of my time . . .'

'I have not!' she burst out hotly.

He glanced pointedly at his watch.

'I will not have you accuse me of lying,' she hissed vehemently. 'Ask your secretary! Ask your cousin! He was there when the message came through. Either you don't communicate clearly, Mr Hunter, or your secretary is somewhat selective in delivering your messages, but don't you dare suggest I'm lying!'

Sparks were flying out of her eyes and they found responsive ground. The grim lines of his expression melted, anger softening into apology.

'Obviously the mistake was not yours, Miss Standish. Please forgive my terseness. I returned to find my secretary absent, you absent, both without explanation, and I'm damnably hungry after a morning of hard bargaining. Do you need to collect any notes, or can you give me a verbal report?'

Jo had been thrown completely off balance. She drew in a deep breath to steady herself. 'Verbal,' she answered briefly, not trusting herself to say more until she had regained control.

'Right, then we'll go.'

He took her arm and steered her back into the elevator. Jo moved like a marionette, stiff and jerky. Michael Hunter pressed the down button, then turned to her with a pleasant smile.

'How did your first week go?'

'Fine,' she clipped out.

'Any problems?'

'No.'

'Complaints?'

'None.'

'All requirements met?'

'Yes.'

His smile widened into an ironic grin. 'Anything you'd like to ask me?'

'No.'

The elevator doors opened and Jo breathed a sigh of relief.

'The restaurant is only a block away, so we'll walk,' he informed her as they emerged on to the sidewalk.

He took her arm again as they weaved through the lunch-hour crowd. Jo concentrated on putting one foot in front of the other. Her brain needed time to get back into efficient working order. Her meetings with Michael Hunter always seemed to be attended by shock and she had invariably defended herself by going on the attack, fighting instinctively to protect herself. He had the disturbing ability to make her feel vulnerable.

She suspected that Susan Trigg had deliberately edited Michael Hunter's message. She remembered the smug spite in her voice and wondered just how well Michael Hunter knew or had known his sexy secretary. Then she remembered Elsie's comments and discarded that idea. Susan Trigg's malice obviously stemmed from dog-in-the-manger frustration. A poor choice as a confidential secretary, Jo thought. Mark's choice, Elsie had said, not Michael Hunter's.

Her glance caught the sign of Danielle's and she was ready for the move towards the staircase leading down. At the lower floor, thick double doors shut out the daylight and city noises. Michael Hunter raised a hand, received a nod of acknowledgement from a waiter, then steered her straight to an empty table for two.

It was the only empty table in the restaurant, Jo noted as she took the chair he held out for her. It had clearly been reserved for them, and it was equally clear that Michael Hunter was well known here. The décor and atmosphere of the restaurant were subdued, businesslike but quietly expensive. The tablecloth was starched white linen and a single red rose stood in a specimen vase. A waiter was quickly on hand with menus and Jo accepted one automatically. She looked down at it and sighed.

'Something the matter?'

She glanced up to meet the questioning blue eyes. 'Mr Hunter, I've already had my lunch,' she stated flatly.

'Have a look anyway. There might be something to tempt you.'

'I'm really not hungry.'

'As you wish,' he shrugged. 'You don't mind if I eat?'

'That's what we're here for,' she retorted sharply, then tempered her answer with stiff politeness. 'I'm sorry you were inconvenienced by the misunderstanding.'

'No matter. Fortunately the service here is fast.'

He signalled the waiter back, gave his order and handed back the menus. Then with an air of satisfaction he sat back and relaxed, his eyes appraising her with warm approval. She fiercely reminded herself who he was, and gradually the warm glow in her blood cooled.

'Shall I begin?' she asked curtly.

He nodded, watching her with keen interest. She began her evaluation of the programmers, shading each assessment with the consideration that their work so far was not conclusive evidence. Michael Hunter nodded to the wine waiter to pour her a glass of claret from the bottle he had ordered, and Jo accepted it without protest. His meal arrived and he ate quietly while she continued her report. He finished at the same time as her closing summary.

'Then you consider that Barry Jensen is the only question mark at this stage,' he remarked, setting his empty plate aside.

Jo frowned. 'So far he's been too conscious of me as a female. It could simply be attention-grabbing tactics. I sorted him out yesterday, so he'll either settle down and produce now or he hasn't got it to produce.'

'Many men have lost their heads around a woman,' he said philosophically, but the gleam in his eyes made it uncomfortably personal.

Jo took refuge in the glass of wine, hiding the leaping confusion in her veins. Damn the man! she thought angrily. I do not want to find him attractive in any shape or form.

A waiter removed his plate and Michael Hunter ordered coffee and crêpes Suzettes for two.

'I told you I wasn't hungry, Mr Hunter,' she reminded him as the waiter departed.

He shrugged. 'They only serve them for two, and I fancied them. You can leave yours on your plate.' His eyes examined her with calculated interest. 'I'm impressed, Miss Standish. That was a very concise and well-reasoned report.'

'Did you expect less?'

He leaned back in his chair, swirled the claret around in his glass, then drank some. As the silence lengthened Jo grew defensive. The unspoken implications that sprang to mind stirred a ready resentment.

'I wasn't sure what to expect. You keep surprising me.' He smiled at her. 'I think you're a very remarkable woman.'

Jo blushed. She was furious with herself, but she blushed. The compliment had completely disarmed her. 'I'm glad you're satisfied,' she mumbled, picking up her own wine-glass as a cover for her agitation.

'And I very much admire your strength of character,' he added softly.

'You surprise me, Mr Hunter. Of any compliment you might choose to pay me, that's the most unexpected.'

His lips lifted in a wry quirk. 'I've long regretted the mistake I made, Miss Standish, but even thinking what I did at the time, I still admired your fierce loyalty to your sister. You had a magnificent dignity —you still do. You won't let anything or anyone put you down. That kind of fighting ability is rare. It takes determination and a strong sense of self-worth. They're qualities you don't meet very often, and when you do, the person is not easily forgotten. I'm glad we've met again.'

Jo frowned. He was throwing her further off balance. It was difficult to hold on to her hostility when the words he spoke were sweet to her ears. She could not think of an adequate reply. Fortunately the waiter returned with a traymobile, then with quick expertise and a dash of theatrical flair he made the sauce and proceeded to serve the crêpes Suzettes. Jo looked down at her plate. The tangy orange aroma teased her appetite.

'They're very good—Danielle's speciality. Why not try one?' Michael Hunter invited offhandedly.

'I think I will,' Jo murmured.

They ate in silence. The sauce was delicious, and Jo gave in to temptation and emptied her plate.

'Mmm, they were good! Just the right amount of Grand Marnier. Sometimes they overdo the liqueur,' she remarked appreciatively before remembering who was sitting opposite her. She looked up and flushed at his smile.

'It seems we have similar tastes.'

'That would be jumping to conclusions, Mr Hunter,' she retorted on a more guarded note.

He made a deliberate action of straightening the cutlery on his plate. 'Your reaction to this luncheon on Monday made me think you might have reacted negatively to my message today. I was wrong, but I know, to my cost, that emotions can override better judgement.'

His gaze swept up to hers, sharply intent as he continued speaking. 'I've made that mistake with tragic results. When you're led to believe a certain thing, and then you're presented with something quite different, the resulting confusion can make you overreact. You do and say things you regret, even as you're saying them. Do you understand what I mean?'

She stared at him blindly, her mind racing back over the past, fitting his words to what had happened. He had believed her when she had confided in him. Then Mark had convinced his cousin that Jo had deliberately deceived him in her version of the affair and he had changed overnight from friend to deadly enemy. Her lips thinned.

'Yes, I understand very well,' she replied grimly.

He frowned at the tone of her answer. The lines of his face became more deeply etched and he looked every year of his age, a dull tiredness dragging at his features. Coffee was served and he took his time adding sugar and stirring it in. He heaved a sigh and gave her a sardonic smile.

'Computers must be easier to work with than human beings. No misunderstandings or breakdowns in communication. Whatever you tell it to do, it does without question.'

'You're quite right,' she shot back at him. 'You can trust computers.'

He paused, taking in the bitter accusation of her eyes. 'But not people?' he asked softly.

'Trust, once lost, never comes again, Mr Hunter,' she stated coldly.

'I agree with you,' he said very deliberately. 'That's why one must be very sure that the whole truth is understood before making such a serious judgement. To get at the truth one should hear and weigh all the evidence.'

It was a calculated challenge. For one moment Jo was tempted to take it up, listen to his justification of actions which could not be justified, and then rip his defence apart. She sighed and shook her head. It would only be dredging up painful memories to no purpose. She and Michael Hunter stood on opposing sides of the fence, Mark Hunter's lies and Carol's death forming an insurmountable barrier. There was no meeting place.

'Mr Hunter, I heard what you had to say three years ago,' she said with quiet insistence, and her eyes held a vulnerable loneliness. 'Nothing you can say now can change the fact of my sister's death.'

Compassion softened his gaze for a brief instant before he glanced down at the coffee-cup in his hand. He toyed absently with the cup, pushing it around its saucer. 'You're right, of course,' he agreed. There was a short silence before he drew in a deep breath and faced her again. 'I've spent many sleepless nights saying "if only", Miss Standish, but all the "if onlys" are not related to my actions. I can say, if only I'd been more controlled that night, if only your sister had been less wilfully determined to have her own way.' He paused and added quietly, 'If only you'd been less innocent, you wouldn't have dismissed me until your sister had tried every feminine wile she could think of to accomplish her purpose.'

Jo recoiled from his words, shaking her head in denial of the suggestion that she was at fault for her sister's death. Wounded green eyes stared their reproach at Michael Hunter, but he continued relentlessly.

'There were two conflicts that night. Your sister's interests was one. You know the other as well as I do. Your pride overrode what your sister wanted, just as my pride demanded retribution for having been misled. Mistakes were made, but if we dwell on "if onlys" we achieve nothing, because you're right —nothing can change the fact of your sister's death. "If only" are two of the most destructive words in the English language. They tempt one into useless dreams, and to brood on the past is to waste the present and the future. Let the past go.'

'Oh, it's so easy for you to say that,' Jo grated. 'I'm sure you dismissed it long ago. Why shouldn't you? It wasn't your family. You can say whatever you like, but I know one thing for certain—if you and your cousin had never entered our lives, Carol would be alive today and I wouldn't be alone. The past holds too many lessons for me to let it go, Mr Hunter, and I'm not dumb. When I learn a lesson I apply it.'

His mouth twisted wryly. 'I would never call you dumb, Miss Standish. I could say blind.'

'Blind!' she flashed back at him. 'Oh yes, blind like people of wealth who only see money!'

A muscle contracted in his cheek, but he held her gaze. 'Blind as in prejudice and hatred,' he said flatly, then leaned forward to speak more persuasively. 'If you must look back, at least open your eyes and see clearly.'

'At this point in time, Mr Hunter, I'm more concerned with the present. You've eaten. I've given you my report.' Jo glanced at her watch. 'It's two o'clock and I should be back at the office. Let's keep to business, shall we?'

Her tone was hard and uncompromising, and Michael Hunter made no demur. He quickly signalled a waiter and handed him a credit card, then he looked back at her with a smile which smacked of satisfaction.

'It's been a very interesting lunch. Perhaps next time we'll get to that unfinished business.'

'What unfinished business?' she asked sharply.

His eyes held a glint of self-mockery as he answered. 'I have a gut feeling that there'll always be unfinished business between us, Miss Standish.' He stood up and held her chair for her. 'At least until we reach an understanding,' he murmured close to her ear as she rose to her feet.

She swung around on him, her eyes denying such a possibility, but his nearness strangled the words on her tongue. She stepped away, disturbed by his physical impact on her, disturbed even more by the almost intimate look in his eyes. 'I doubt that, Mr Hunter,' she managed weakly, then turned to make her way towards the exit.

She was very aware of him following her, knew exactly when he paused for the return of his credit card. Another waiter held the door open and she kept going up the stairs without looking back. Michael Hunter's touch on her elbow brought a falter to her step. He loomed up beside her and kept a light hold as they walked back to the office.

'It looks as if the weather will hold for the weekend. Got anything planned?' he remarked casually.

'Yes,' Jo replied, hard purpose in her voice as she

thought of Mark Hunter.

'With someone?'

She darted him a suspicious glance, but his expression was bland. He could not possibly know about Mark's party invitation. 'That's my private business, Mr Hunter.'

'Just making polite conversation, Miss Standish.'

She looked stonily ahead. They reached the office building and Jo gave a sigh of relief as she saw that an elevator was immediately available. The sooner she was away from Michael Hunter the better; he was too dangerous to her peace of mind. He pressed the appropriate buttons and stood beside her in the small compartment, again making her feel claustrophobic.

'Are you happy with him?'

'With whom?' she retorted sharply, wishing he would keep silent and leave her alone.

'The man in your life.'

'You're jumping to conclusions again, Mr Hunter,' she said coldly.

'Meaning there's no particular man?'

'Meaning it's my private business.'

'Yes, but it's an interesting speculation,' he grinned, unabashed by her stiffness. 'A woman of your calibre wouldn't be easily satisfied.'

The elevator doors opened on to the computer floor, and Jo gave him a slight nod and stepped out.

She settled down to work, but again she found it difficult to concentrate. Michael Hunter's words kept trampling through her mind. She wondered if he truly admired her. His sincerity had to be suspect, but they had been pleasing compliments, more pleasing than any she had ever received. If only . . .

she pulled herself up. Michael Hunter had been right about those words. They were deadly. She would not think of 'if onlys'. She would deal with life as it came, and the most immediate thing was work. She would work and put everything else out of her mind.

CHAPTER SIX

THE white chiffon dress was elegant and feminine with its low V-neckline and flowing skirt. Jo clipped on the plaited gold necklet that matched the woven belt. She slipped her feet into finely strapped sandals then examined the full effect of her appearance in the mirror. It was an outfit which would pass anywhere in any company. Not only pass, she thought mockingly. She would stand out with her height. Mark Hunter's friends were sure to be stylish but she would not be outshone.

The doorbell rang and Jo grimaced. She no longer had the heart for the charade she had planned. Nothing she could do would help Carol now. Mark Hunter would remain Mark Hunter, and revenge was a waste of time and emotion. She had her own life to live, but at least tonight she could make sure that Mark Hunter would not pester her again with his unwanted attentions. His persistance would be brought to an abrupt end.

'You look absolutely stunning!' he greeted her and she recoiled inwardly from the speculative glitter in his eyes.

'Thank you,' she said with cold politeness. 'I'm afraid I'm not quite ready. Would you like to come in for a minute?'

He was only too pleased. She deliberately refrained from offering him a drink and having excused herself she hurried back to her bedroom to organise her evening bag. It took very little time to put in cosmetics, tissues and handkerchief. Jo was annoyed with herself for not having done it before. She had not intended Mark to stray into her home—not that she was in any way ashamed of it. On the contrary, she was very content with what she had.

Her eyes swept around the bedroom. She loved the browns and cream and peach tonings in this room. They were soft, and warm and restful. She had bought herself a double bed to accommodate her length more comfortably and the printed quilt that lay on top of the brown satin under-frill still delight-ed her eye, peach-blossoms with their brown twigs giving it a slightly eastern look. She checked her appearance in the mirror once more, wished she was staying at home, then with a resigned sigh, flicked off the overhead light and returned to the living-room.

It was a spacious room and Jo had filled it with much-loved possessions. She did not have original paintings on the walls, but she doubted that even Michael Hunter could afford the originals of the Cézanne and Gauguin prints she had chosen.

Mark suddenly looked up and saw her. 'I notice you have some tapes of James Galway. Fantastic on the flute, isn't he?'

'Yes,' Jo replied briefly, surprised by the comment but disinclined to encourage a discussion. 'I'm ready now. I'm sorry for keeping you waiting.'

'No matter,' he smiled, then gestured around him appreciatively. 'I've enjoyed myself. This room has tremendous warmth and personality. I can see you've been hiding from me, Jo.'

'Hiding? Since you've known where to find me all week I can't be accused of hiding.'

He looked at her bemusedly as she swept past him and opened the door.

'Coming?' she added pointedly.

He hesitated, drawing something from his pocket. 'I've just broken the band on my watch. Would you mind if I left it here for safe keeping? I wouldn't like to lose it.'

'Leave it here.' She indicated the table by the door, suspecting it might be an excuse to enter her apartment later. 'Don't forget about it, will you?'

'No chance,' he grinned, and Jo knew that her suspicion was justified.

Once in his car and on their way, Mark set himself to be entertaining, but she gave little in the way of response. Much of what he said was amusing and she admitted to herself that she would probably have been amused if he was not Mark Hunter. It was a relief to reach their destination. She did not want to be alone with him.

The size of the house and grounds indicated that his friends were very wealthy. Jo had anticipated that. Everything about Mark Hunter, his clothes, his manner, his arrogance, branded him as one of the privileged class. He would never have married a common shopgirl, not even one as pretty as Carol.

They were met at the door by an attractive, vivacious woman whose words tumbled over each other and whose eyes missed nothing. Jo felt she had been printed and classified at one sharp glance. When Mark was able to interrupt the bubbling welcome he introduced her.

'Peg, I'd like you to meet Jo Standish. Jo, our irrepressible hostess, Peg McAlister.'

'How do you do,' Jo smiled.

'Jo? My goodness. I thought you'd be a Justine or a Claudette or at least a Charmain! Your name doesn't fit at all,' Peg declared so amusingly that Jo had to smile.

'Peg prides herself on being able to pigeonhole people. She thinks you're a model,' Mark explained teasingly.

'Well, you do have a weakness for models, Mark, and Jo certainly has the style. I can't be far wrong,' Peg retorted archly.

'I'm afraid you are this time,' Jo told her. 'I'm doing computer work for Hunt's at the moment.'

'My God—brains too! Lead her in, Mark, before I shrivel up with an inferiority complex. And don't be selfish! Introduce her around.'

There was no trace of envy in her voice. The lighthearted banter was designed to put Jo at ease, and it achieved its purpose. Then just as Mark steered her through an archway Peg called after them.

'Oh, is Mike coming, do you know?'

Jo froze. Did she mean Michael Hunter? Mark shrugged, so that as they moved forward again she felt compelled to settle the uncertainty.

'Mike who?' she asked offhandedly.

'My cousin, of course,' Mark answered a little sardonically. 'But he won't come—Mike hates parties. He always wriggles out of them.'

The relief was enormous. The idea of coming face to face with Michael Hunter while she was in Mark's company was too discomforting to dwell upon. Their host called them over to a bar in one corner of the large entertainment room, and Jo was only too glad to be distracted. She asked for fruit juice, despite

Mark's sceptical protest.

'Jo?'

'Sorry, Mark. What did you say?'

'There are some friends over there I'd like you to meet.'

She nodded and slid off her stool. 'Thanks, Charlie,' she smiled over her shoulder as Mark took her arm in a proprietary manner.

'Mark Hunter!' someone shrilled from across the room.

'Oh God—Margot Sharmon!' Mark muttered in disgust.

A very bejewelled woman detached herself from a group of people and descended on them. 'Fancy seeing you here! Looking as handsome as ever, I see.' Jo was treated to a feline stare. 'And how's dear Barbara?'

'Dear Barbara is tripping around Europe with her new husband,' Mark replied with a weary sigh.

'I'm so sorry,' Margot gushed. 'I had no idea. You always looked so beautiful together.'

'Yes—well, I'm told that looks aren't everything.' His eyes twinkled at Jo. 'And perhaps I prefer a woman of character. What do you think, Jo?'

'I don't think character alone would attract you.'

'Ah, but you're a harsh judge, my sweet.'

'And you're a hypocrite, Mark Hunter,' the other woman accused. 'I've never seen you passing the time with a plain woman yet. But that's beside the point. What are you doing in Sydney?'

'Working. What else?'

'That reminds me—is Mike here too?'

'I haven't seen him.'

'He's so wretchedly elusive!' Margot sighed in

vexation. 'I must ask Peg about him.'

As she trailed off in an expensive cloud of perfume, Mark's lips curled in derision. 'Bitch! She knew damned well we were divorced. I'm glad it's Mike she's aiming to get her claws into instead of me. Sorry, Jo—Margot's a cat of the highest order.'

'Is your cousin interested?' The question was out before Jo could call back the words.

'Mike? Not likely. Women fawn all over him, but he's pretty cagey. Doesn't take anyone seriously.'

Mark steered her through the crowd of milling guests and out on to an extensive patio which encompassed a sparkling swimming pool. Chinese lanterns hung from various trees in the landscaped gardens, adding to the festive atmosphere. Mark was immediately hailed by a group of friends who loudly welcomed both of them into their circle.

Jo had little time to acclimatise herself to names and faces. Someone turned up the music which suddenly throbbed out in an insistent disco beat, and the group split up as couples were urged into dancing. Jo was reluctant to join them, but Mark would not take a refusal. He pulled her towards a clear area and swung straight into the rhythm, his movements sensuous and completely uninhibited. She reacted by becoming stiff and wooden, repelled by the intimacy of the dance.

'Loosen up, Jo,' he urged.

'I told you I was no good at it.'

'Just let yourself go.'

'I never let myself go, Mark,' she replied tersely.

He cocked an eyebrow at her. 'That sounds challenging. Of course fruit juice doesn't help. What you need is some warm alcohol in your veins.'

'You could be right,' Jo agreed. 'let's see if that bar over there can provide the necessary.'

Anything was preferable to dancing with him. A temporary bar had been set up next to the swimming pool, and Jo walked towards it, taking Mark's acceptance for granted. There were bottles of champagne nestling in a tub of ice and Mark wasted no time in uncorking one. He handed her a brimming glass and was about to fill one for himself when he was grabbed from behind in an exuberant hug.

'Oh no, you don't! I'm here to claim my duty dance,' Peg McAlister grinned over his shoulder.

'Uh-uh,' Mark declined firmly, ignoring her. 'Later, Peg. I was just oiling Jo up so she could perform.'

Peg refused to let go. 'No dice! This one's mine. You can dance with Jo for the rest of the night. My time's limited. You don't mind, do you, Jo?'

'Of course not,' she smiled, only too happy to pass Mark on to anyone.

'Besides, I've brought Mike over to keep you company.'

Mark turned in astonishment. 'Good God! Don't tell me you got him here!'

Jo turned much more slowly, trying to combat the hollow feeling in her stomach. He was just behind her. The blue eyes seemed to mock her gently as he replied to Mark's show of disbelief.

'Nothing would have kept me away from . . . this party,' he said slowly, the words accented with meaning.

'Then why did I have to scold you into it, you anti-social brute!' Peg pouted at him.

'I'm here, Peg. Since you seem to think that's a

matter for satisfaction, you should be content. Now, why don't you two go off and enjoy yourselves,' he commanded quietly.

Mark cast a half-gaping look of surprise, but he did as he was told, urged on by an eager Peg. Jo watched them go. Just like puppets, she thought with sinking dismay. Michael Hunter seemed to exert authority wherever he was, arranging everything how he saw fit. The fact that he had arranged to be alone with her now set her nerves on edge.

She found herself clutching the glass of champagne too tightly and took a quick gulp to fortify herself. She would not let Michael Hunter intimidate her, whatever he had to say. She turned to face him, a defiant challenge in her eyes.

'You're looking very beautiful tonight.'

It sounded so trite and commonplace that Jo almost laughed. Then she remembered how those blue eyes had dismissed her three years ago and she did laugh. He raised a quizzical eyebrow.

'I wasn't expecting you to say that.'

'Why not? It's true.'

She shrugged and a cynical smile curved her lips. 'It's amazing what a modelling school can do, even with ordinary clay.'

Her words had more impact than she had anticipated. Michael stiffened and a cold hardness crept over his features.

'I'm more interested in the person, not the façade.'

'I'm well aware that looks are unimportant, Mr Hunter, unless you want to get on in the world. It was you who placed the emphasis on my appearance.'

'I'm rarely impressed by appearances. I've met

too many beautiful women who have nothing to offer but their sex appeal. And you're quite right, they do get on in the world,' he said harshly.

'Have you ever wondered what happens to the non-beautiful people, Mr Hunter? But of course, you couldn't possibly imagine.' Her eyes swept over him in deliberate appraisal, noting the expensive silk of his brown shirt and the tailored fit of his cream linen slacks. 'You're a beautiful person yourself, aren't you? You've probably never appreciated how useful it is to be attractive, how many doors it opens . . .'

'How many bedrooms it gets you into?'

Hot colour scorched her cheeks as she raked him with fiercely proud eyes. 'I hope you're referring to yourself.'

Suddenly he smiled, his eyes warming perceptibily as they gazed into hers. 'No bedrooms for you, Jo?'

The complete turnabout in tone and manner flustered her. Before she could make any response he had taken her arm and was drawing her towards some deck-chairs on the nearby lawn.

'Let's not waste any more time. I want to talk to you,' he said purposefully.

Jo stopped dead and refused to budge any further. 'And what if I don't want to talk to you? This isn't business hours, you know,' she said mutinously.

'Please?'

He smiled again and Jo had no defence ready. He was the most attractive man she had ever met and despite all the pitfalls that his company implied, she allowed herself to be seated in a deck-chair next to him. Almost instantly she began chiding herself for stupidity.

'Do you like parties?' he asked with a sardonic lilt

'Sometimes they can be amusing,' she answered briefly.

'I don't care for crowds when I'm in the company of a woman I like.'

'Oh? I suppose you'd wine and dine her in an intimate little setting.'

'Not necessarily, but that would be a decided improvement on this.'

'Well, apparently you have plenty of women to choose from.' She gestured airily towards the dancers on the patio. 'I'm told they run after you in droves.'

Her hand had barely come to rest again when it was taken up by a larger, stronger hand. Fingers curled possessively around hers and for one insane moment she had the impression they were clutching her heart, squeezing it, claiming ownership. A vibrant electricity was coursing up her arm and her head jerked towards Michael Hunter, her eyes snapping a startled protest. It never reached her lips. His gaze captured hers, seducing all words from her tongue. He was demanding an acknowledgement of the attraction between them, and time was whirling backwards and it was as if they were facing each other in his apartment with that silent, magical communication piercing their souls.

'You're the woman of my choice, Jo.'

The words were soft, intimate, their message a joyous beat in her heart, a song of elation in her blood, dancing a wildly exciting tempo all the way up to her brain where a shattering denial rolled their meaning away like a drum sounding a death-tattoo.

'No.' The mournful negative echoed faintly on her

lips as panic grew in her mind. No—not him! She could not let him—never. It was madness to even recognise that message, let alone admit it to her heart. She wrenched her gaze away and snatched her hand out of his. In miserable agitation she rubbed at her hand, desperate to remove the spell he had cast. She sucked in her breath, held it for several seconds and let it out slowly, battling hard against her renegade emotions. A hand touched her arm in a soft caress and she flinched away.

'You know it's true,' he insisted quietly.

'Look elsewhere, Michael Hunter,' she ordered harshly. 'You've made an impossible choice.'

'I don't accept the word impossible. Difficult, yes, but if you can accept Mark's company, why not mine?'

'It amuses me to accept Mark's company,' she answered coldly.

'Don't play with revenge, Jo. It sours the spirit. If it's amusement you want, amuse yourself with me.'

Forcing a mask of indifference over her face, she turned to him and very deliberately held his gaze. 'You don't amuse me.'

'I'm glad you feel that,' he declared softly. 'I'm glad you can't laugh me off, because it's no laughing matter to me. I want you to spend tomorrow with me and we'll settle the past once and for all, get it out of the way.'

'No!'

The word was a protest, sharp and emotional. His eyes narrowed on the brief flicker of vulnerability and he spoke with more determination.

'Yes, Jo. I'm not going to give up and go away. You and I have much to say to each other and I'll keep on at you until I'm satisfied that the situation between us has been resolved, one way or the other. Give me tomorrow. If by the end of the day we haven't reached an understanding, I won't press you any more.'

'Why should I give you anything? Why should I believe your word? Tell me that,' she demanded hotly, trying to repress the panic which was creating havoc in her veins.

'Because basically you're a fair person and I wouldn't be pressing you if I didn't have something to prove. I want your time and your company, Jo, but if I can't persuade you into giving them to me freely by the end of tomorrow, then you're not the woman I think you are. I'll have no reason to pursue anything but business with you.'

Her eyes questioned his sincerity. His gaze remained steadfast, persuasive in its intensity. One day. The temptation was strong. Suddenly she wanted to hear what he had to say. The emotions he aroused in her needed to be sorted out. Either her hostility was firmly based or . . . She frowned and looked away. He was dangerous.

'Well, is it a bargain?'

The soft voice caressed her ears, seducing her with its reasonable request. 'All right—one day. But I doubt you can change my mind about anything, Michael Hunter.'

'We'll see.'

She could hear the smile in his voice and again she felt a surge of panic. Mindless panic, she reasoned firmly. He could get no closer to her than she would let him, and she would keep a safe distance between herself and Michael Hunter. It was only one day.

Say Hello to Yesterday
Holly Weston had done it all alone.

She had raised her small son and worked her way up to features writer for a major newspaper. Still the bitterness of the the past seven years lingered.

She had been very young when she married Nick Falconer—but old enough to lose her heart completely when he left. Despite her success in her new life, her old one haunted her.

But it was over and done with—until an assignment in Greece brought her face to face with Nick, and all she was trying to forget. . . .

Time of the Temptress
The game must be played his way!

Rebellion against a cushioned, controlled life had landed Eve Tarrant in Africa. Now only the tough mercenary Wade O'Mara stood between her and possible death in the wild, revolution-torn jungle.

But the real danger was Wade himself—he had made Eve aware of herself as a woman.

"I saved your neck, so you feel you owe me something," Wade said. "But you don't owe me a thing, Eve. Get away from me." She knew she could make him lose his head if she tried. But that wouldn't solve anything. . . .

Your Romantic Adventure Starts Here.

Born Out of Love
It had to be coincidence!

Charlotte stared at the man through a mist of confusion. It was Logan. An older Logan, of course, but unmistakably the man who had ravaged her emotions and then abandoned her all those years ago.

She ought to feel angry. She ought to feel resentful and cheated. Instead, she was apprehensive—terrified at the complications he could create.

"We are not through, Charlotte," he told her flatly. "I sometimes think we haven't even begun."

Man's World
Kate was finished with love for good.

Kate's new boss, features editor Eliot Holman, might have devastating charms—but Kate couldn't care less, even if it was obvious that he was interested in her.

Everyone, including Eliot, thought Kate was grieving over the loss of her husband, Toby. She kept it a carefully guarded secret just how cruelly Toby had treated her and how terrified she was of trusting men again.

But Eliot refused to leave her alone, which only served to infuriate her. He was no different from any other man. . . or was he?

These FOUR free Harlequin Presents novels allow you to enter the world of romance, love and desire. As a member of the Harlequin Home Subscription Plan, you can continue to experience all the moods of love. You'll be inspired by moments so real...so moving...you won't want them to end. So start your own Harlequin Presents adventure by returning the reply card below. <u>DO IT TODAY!</u>

EXTRA BONUS
MAIL YOUR ORDER
TODAY AND GET A
FREE TOTE BAG
FROM HARLEQUIN.

'Do you enjoy sailing?' he asked interestedly.

'I don't know. I've never been.'

'Then it should be a pleasant experience for you. We'll go out on the Harbour for the day. There's nothing like a fresh breeze in your face to make you clear-headed.'

'Oh, I'll keep a very clear head,' she retorted mockingly. A ripple of apprehension darted through her as she suddenly realised that a boat on the Harbour formed a very effective prison. He was ensuring that they would be very alone together. 'Will there be other people on this boat?' she asked as calmly as she could.

'No. I can handle it myself.'

'I'm not sure sailing is a good idea. I might get sick,' she said indecisively.

'I won't take you into rough waters. Don't worry, Jo. I'll take very good care of you. I want you to enjoy yourself.'

She glanced at him warily, but his eyes were glowing with warmth that reached out and encompassed her. Her resistance was melting, and she stiffened her backbone.

'I don't expect to enjoy myself. I simply want to be finished with you,' she insisted defensively.

'Now you're jumping to conclusions,' he smiled. 'Keep an open mind, Jo. Tomorrow belongs to the future.'

'I thought you wanted to discuss the past.'

'To begin with, yes, but that's not all I want. Give me your address and I'll pick you up at nine o'clock.'

She gave it to him without argument, almost fatalistically. If Michael Hunter was so determined he would keep pressuring her in one way or another.

It was better to get it settled. She tried to appraise him objectively as he wrote her address down. He was a man who had everything at his fingertips, so what did he want with her? He glanced up, caught her curious scrutiny and raised a quizzical eyebrow.

'Why haven't you married?' she asked bluntly.

'Why haven't you?'

She shrugged. 'I'm rather wary when it comes to commitments. I'm also old-fashioned enough to want a marriage that will last.'

'Precisely my own view. Divorce is too messy.' He put his notebook away, then grinned his satisfaction at her. 'I have a feeling that we have a lot of views in common.'

'I wouldn't bet on it,' Jo said drily.

'You dance like a maniac, Peg!'

Mark's laughing voice came as a welcome distraction. Michael Hunter's presence was tempting her on to treacherous ground.

'Your fault, darling. You inspire me,' Peg retorted before raising her voice in salute. 'Well, you two, I hope you're not going to be lounge-lizards all evening.'

'Each to his own, Peg,' Michael Hunter observed drily as he rose to his feet and offered her his chair. 'Sit down and rest your weary bones for a while.'

'Only if you bring me some champagne.' She dropped into the chair and grinned up at him. 'You do owe me a favour.'

'Coming right up!'

'Bring a whole bottle,' Mark called after his departing figure. He had been busy drawing up extra chairs, but now he was eager to claim Jo's attention. 'Sorry I was so long, but Peg wouldn't let up.'

'Just listen to him!' Peg scoffed. 'He loved every minute of it, and if you say anything else, Mark, I warn you, I'll take offence and not feed you.'

He threw up his hands in mock dismay. 'I'm warned! You were brilliant! She was brilliant, wasn't she, Jo?'

'You were both brilliant. I don't know how you do it. I'm hopeless.'

'Don't tell me you were watching. Was Mike boring you to tears on the subject of work?' Peg remarked sceptically.

'No. He didn't even mention it.'

'Come off it, Peg,' Mark put in derisively. 'You know damned well Mike can be just as civilised as anyone when he puts his mind to it.'

'Civilised! Let me tell you, Mark Hunter, none of us is civilised when it comes to getting what we want. Mike is a prime example of that, wouldn't you say, Jo?'

'Lay off, Peg. This is only the second time they've met,' said Mark with a mild show of irritation.

'Is that so? And when was the first?'

'At a business meeting, the same as me. Isn't that right, Jo?'

She hesitated, not wanting to lie, but even more reluctant to feed Peg's avid interest. 'Not quite. We met very briefly before, but we weren't properly introduced.'

Mike was approaching with a bottle of champagne and a handful of glasses. The diversion was timely. There was something niggling about Peg's questions.

'Here you are,' he said with a flourish, handing around the glasses and filling them.

'Mmm! Just what I need,' Peg purred appreciatively. 'When did you first meet Jo, Mike?'

There was only the minutest hesitation before he sighed with apparent exasperation. 'Peg! You're an endearing lady, a charming hostess and an inveterate gossip. I refuse to answer your question on the grounds that . . .'

'It will incriminate you,' Peg finished smugly.

'No, on the grounds that my answer will spoil the enjoyment you get from speculating. The simple truth would ruin your night.'

Mark burst out laughing and even Jo had to smile at the cleverness of his sidestep. They had been a few tense moments for her.

'You see,' he continued, tongue in cheek, 'Mark doesn't mind creating gossip at all, but I have a passion for privacy which parties don't respect. You scold me for being a reluctant guest, so I come. Then you set about doing the one thing I abhor.' He shook his head at her and subsided into a chair. 'I can see you don't want me here again.'

'Mike Hunter, you dare to blackmail me!' she started threateningly.

'Give over, Peg,' Mark grinned at her. 'He's got you fair and square. How many people can boast of getting him to a party? Your friend Margot will be ever so grateful to you.'

Mike groaned. 'Not Margot Sharmon again!'

'And you be polite to her too, you cruel, heartless beast. Since you won't let me gossip, I suppose I'd better see about supper. Are you all starving?'

'Ravenous!' Mark declared feelingly.

'Oh, you'd gobble anything up. Jo, would you mind giving me a hand for ten minutes?'

'Hey, hold on,' Mark protested. 'You haul me off to dance and I just get my girl back and you start hauling her off! Have a heart, Peg!'

'Serves you right for being greedy.'

Jo had risen to her feet and Peg linked her arm companionably to hers.

'I think we'll go while we're winning, Jo. You two can finish the champagne, consolation for our absence.'

Peg hustled her off towards the kitchen, keeping up a non-stop flow of trivial comments. Jo was not sure if she had been rescued or shanghaied. She was grateful for the escape from the Hunter men, but Peg's itch for gossip made her a formidable companion. Her hostess organised her into buttering slices of French bread, then began checking various dishes. Before Jo could become complacent with the situation, Peg fired at point-blank range.

'Well, I sure had you misplaced! Underneath that cool exterior must lurk a femme fatale. You've got Mark drooling at the mouth and Mike in an absolute flap! How do you do it?'

'That's a wild exaggeration,' Jo smiled, and kept on buttering bread.

'Not a bit of it!' Peg declared with confidence. 'Mark usually flirts around with everyone at parties, but I had a hard time keeping him dancing while you were with Mike. He's smitten all right.'

'It's probably because I'm new. It won't last,' Jo replied carelessly.

'I don't know about that, but I'd like to know how you got your hooks into Mike. He's been palming women off for years. Never in my whole life have I seen him actually run after one.'

'I hardly think one conversation constitutes running after me.'

'Ah, but it's what led up to the conversation that's so intriguing,' Peg announced with gleeful triumph.

'I'm afraid you've lost me,' Jo told her.

'I don't think so,' Peg retorted archly. 'You weren't expecting to see him, were you?'

'No.'

'And he wasn't expecting you to be with Mark.'

'I wouldn't think so,' Jo answered more cautiously.

'And he didn't like it one bit, did he?'

A warning tingled up Jo's spine. 'I don't know what you mean,' she said offhandedly.

'Well, if you were trying to make him jealous, you certainly succeeded. He reacted so fast I wouldn't have believed it if I hadn't seen it. Mike Hunter running after a woman!' Peg shook her head in amazement. 'When I think of how many traps poor Margot has set for him, not to mention all the other hopefuls trying their hand, and you walk in as cool as a cucumber and scoop the pool.'

'Look,' Jo broke in impatiently, 'you're making something out of nothing.'

'Uh-uh,' Peg denied knowingly. 'There's something going on all right. I telephoned Mike when he didn't look like turning up tonight. He offered belated apologies, but I was annoyed with him for letting me down. I told him that if Mark could turn up with a ravishing brunette from work, I didn't see why he couldn't make the effort. The silence from his end was positively electric. Then he asked for your name, and again there was an awful silence. You could feel the tension right along the line. Then he said he would come. Now, if that isn't drawing power, I don't know what is!'

She waited expectantly for Jo to respond, but was disappointed. The only visible reaction to her words was the sudden stillness of the knife in Jo's hand. She had stopped buttering.

All arranged. All very neatly arranged. Any revenge effectively diverted, Jo reasoned, her sanity completely restored. It was very clear now, now that she was removed from the emotional confusion that Mike Hunter stirred. His words and actions all had one purpose. Separate Jo Standish from Mark. Avert any possible problem.

'Well?' Peg prompted.

'Well what?' Jo said tightly.

'You can't tell me all that single-minded purpose was for nothing,' Peg said insistently.

'Oh, it wasn't for nothing,' Jo retorted with heavy irony. 'It just achieved nothing, that's all.'

'Are you crazy or something?' Peg squeaked in frustration. 'You mean he rushed over here, angled to get you away from Mark, and you knocked him back?'

'You've got it all wrong, Peg. Michael Hunter doesn't want me. And I certainly don't want him,' Jo stated grimly.

Peg looked at her with incredulous eyes. 'Are you mad? Not want that gorgeous hunk of man? What more could you want? Don't tell me you prefer Mark.'

Jo gave a derisive laugh. 'No, I don't want him either. My only form of madness was to get involved with the Hunters socially. I should have known better.' She sighed. 'You've got hold of a red herring,

Peg. It leads nowhere. Please excuse me.'

Fool, fool fool! The word pounded on Jo's brain as she made her escape to the powder room. Hadn't Michael shown her that his word could not be trusted? She knew that. She knew that, and yet she had listened to him.

Vanity, she thought derisively as she eyed herself in the mirror. She touched up her make-up, adding a bit of much-needed colour. He had only wanted to distract her from pursuing any revenge until Mark was safely back in Melbourne. 'Let me amuse you,' he had said quite openly. She had only been deluding herself about attracting him. Michael Hunter only saw her as trouble and he had set out to defuse that trouble.

The cynical play on her emotions made her seethe. She would rejoin the party, seek him out and throw his sailing invitation back in his face. Then she would ask Mark to take her home. Heartsick and weary, all she wanted now was to be finished with the Hunters. Business might preclude that for a while, but in any personal sense, they were anathema to her.

CHAPTER SEVEN

'AT last!' Mark pounced on her. 'I've been sending everyone away from our table. They can eat standing up—we're going to sit in comfort and enjoy our food in a civilised manner. I've got it all set up.'

He hurried her over to a small table which was loaded with a variety of delicacies. Most of the guests were milling around a sumptuous buffet, but Mark was intent on getting Jo alone. The arrangement suited her for the time being. The table gave her a handy vantage point to watch out for Michael Hunter.

He was easily spotted. He did not move around much. People gravitated to him, especially women. Despite her frequent glances at him, never once did she catch his eye on her. If Jo had needed proof that his interest was bogus, this was conclusive. He obviously thought he had achieved his aim and did not bother reinforcing the fact.

'Jo?' The impatient note in Mark's voice warned her that she had been caught wanting, but he followed her line of vision and began chuckling. 'Just look at the boredom on Mike's face, will you? Margot Sharmon is fighting a losing battle.'

It was quite true, but Jo was not amused. She was formulating a plan which would wipe that look of boredom off his face.

Time dragged. It was increasingly difficult to maintain any show of interest in Mark's conversation. Everything about him irritated her, and her nerves were already rubbed raw. Her attention kept drifting to Michael Hunter.

Then suddenly he was gone. Without so much as a wave in their direction he was gone. Jo burned with frustration. Now she was faced with an unpleasant scene in the morning, but at least this charade with Mark could be ended—right now.

'I'm rather tired, Mark,' she said abruptly, cutting into his monologue. 'Do you think we could go?'

'Of course,' he smiled, and Jo winced inwardly at the eagerness in his eyes. She wished fervently that she had not come to this party.

They went about their leavetaking with a minimum of fuss. Peg McAlister looked oddly at her, but Jo assured her hostess that she had enjoyed her hospitality. It was a blessed relief to step out into the cooler night air and know she was going home.

The drive home seemed mercifully short. Mark seemed as preoccupied as she, not attempting any conversation. He escorted Jo to her apartment and waited while she unlocked the front door. She knew he expected to be invited in, but she had no intention of letting the evening drag on any further. Enough was enough. She did not want revenge, she only wanted to be rid of him. With a stiff little smile, she turned back to him and offered her hand.

'Goodnight, Mark. Thank you for a pleasant evening.'

'Goodnight?' He glanced at her hand and then back to her face as if it had to be a joke.

'Yes, goodnight,' she repeated firmly, pushing the door open and stepping inside.

'Now, hold on a minute, Jo! That's a bit abrupt,

even for you. What's this supposed to mean in your book of rules?'

She looked at him wearily. 'Mark, I'm tired, very tired. I don't want to argue with you. I simply want to close this door and go to bed . . . alone,' she added meaningfully.'Now will you please say goodnight and go.'

'No, dammit! Just give me a minute, for God's sake!'

He pushed his way in and shut the door firmly behind him. Jo had stepped back, but now she stood her ground and glared at him resentfully.

'I did not invite you in,' she said icily. 'There's no point in an unpleasant scene. Please go, and don't bother me again, Mark.'

He spread his hands in exasperation, his eyes suddenly pleading with her. 'Look, what do you think I am—a two-bit Casanova? Is that it?'

'That's about it,' she confirmed, too fed up with the Hunters to mince her words.

'Why?' He shook his head in puzzlement. 'I haven't come on strong. Not a word out of place. What have I done wrong?'

Jo heaved an impatient sigh. 'Mark, you've pestered me all week without getting any encouragement for your attentions. You asked me to give this party a try and I have. Now, that's it. No more. Goodnight and goodbye.'

Jo knew she had gone beyond what was acceptable. She was not being at all civil, but this was her home, not an office, and Mark Hunter deserved no sensitivity from her either.

'Then why the hell did you accept? You'd already said no often enough. Why did you give me any hope?' he demanded angrily.

'Hope!' Jo repeated contemptuously. 'There was never any hope for you, Mark Hunter. I accepted your invitation simply to get you off my back. You were sticking like a leech.'

His hand snaked out and grabbed her arm, pulling her against him before she could react. He held her with cruel strength, so closely she could hardly breathe.

'Like a leech, eh?' he mocked savagely. 'So, tonight was all one goddamned tease! I never had a chance.' His eyes glittered down at her and he made a harsh, derisive sound. 'Mike always told me I was a rotten judge of women, but I thought you were different, Jo. In a class of your own, I thought. Not like my bitch of a wife . . .'

'Let me go!' Jo demanded angrily, furious with him and herself for letting the situation get out of hand.

But he held her more forcibly so that he could raise a hand to her throat. With insulting deliberation he trailed light fingers down the V-neckline of her dress and brushed across the revealing swell of breasts. Before Jo could say another word he swooped, grinding his mouth inexorably against hers in a punishing intimacy which could not be called a kiss. She tried to twist her head away, but he held her neck in a vicelike grip. She gritted her teeth to frustrate his savage onslaught and managed to free an arm, then she whipped it up and hit him with all her strength. The resounding crack on his face produced the desired effect. He reeled away from her, his hand moving instinctively to cover the smarting ear and eye.

'Get out! Get out!' Jo screeched at him, her chest heaving in rage. 'I hate you, do you hear? I loathe your touch. I can't bear you near me. Get out!'

'I'm going,' Mark snarled. 'The feeling's mutual.'

He wrenched the door open and slammed it behind him. Jo stood there, quivering with the force of her revulsion. Tears gathered in her eyes and began a slow trickle down her cheeks. All the twisted emotions of the night formed a painful knot in her stomach and she headed blindly for her bedroom, needing to lie down and lick her wounds. She automatically slid off her clothes, throwing them carelessly on a chair, not even bothering to drag on a nightie before climbing between the sheets and burying her head in a pillow.

She should have walked out of Michael Hunter's office last Monday and never looked back. Pride had made her stay and face them, pride and a fierce determination to prove they could not hurt her any more. But they could. And they had.

Mark Hunter would keep away now. That at least had been achieved, Jo thought bitterly. Tomorrow morning she would get rid of Michael Hunter.

Thoroughly miserable in spite of her resolutions, Jo slowly drifted into sleep, but even her sleep brought torment. Nightmarish dreams made her restless, elusive shadows teasing at her mind, all the more harrowing for not being clear-cut.

She awoke, gasping for breath and flailing her arms. The restless tossing had twisted the bed-sheet around her body, hot and confining. Having untangled herself, she staggered off to the bathroom. The mirror told her she was a mess, her face streaked with make-up, her hair still half pinned up. Tiredly she creamed her face and rinsed it in cold water. Her head was aching. She removed the rest of her hairpins, cursing herself for drinking too much champagne during the latter half of the party. It had helped wash Mark's company down, but she regretted it now.

She downed two aspirins and stumbled back to bed, exhausted and resentful that her sleep had been broken. Thoughts of Mark and Mike Hunter jumbled around in her mind until she slept again.

This time Michael Hunter was standing on a boat. He was smiling and beckoning to her to step aboard. She was about to take that step when Mark appeared at his cousin's shoulder, a triumphant leer on his face. She hesitated and they both urged her to come. Suddenly there was a squeal of brakes, a scream. Jo turned to see Carol's broken body on the road and a terrible buzzing filled her head. She put her hands over her ears to stop it, rolling her head from side to side. She heard her voice crying, 'No, no, no!' and forced herself awake.

The doorbell was buzzing insistently. Jo felt completely disoriented, unable to think or act. Her eyes focussed on the clock. Eight-fifty-five. Memory jolted her upright. Michael Hunter was at the door. She swung her legs to the floor and sat for a moment, her head in her hands. The ringing stopped and then started again. Michael Hunter was not going to conveniently drift away. Jo dragged herself up and slid her arms into a cotton housecoat, then ran a brush through her tangled hair, tossed the long tresses back over her shoulders and fastened the wrap-around tie of her housecoat. She gave herself a defiant look in the mirror, lifted her chin and marched out to answer the door, determined to send Michael Hunter on his way.

'I was beginning to wonder if I had the right apartment number.'

The casual greeting was attended by a smile, but Jo stared stonily back, unmoved by the handsome figure he cut in his white jeans and navy T-shirt. He was a perfect advertisement for the great outdoors, a prime example of sun-bronzed virility, but she stubbornly clung to her resolve to have no part of him.

'I overslept,' she said bluntly. 'In fact you just woke me up.'

'I'm sorry. Can I get you some breakfast while you get ready?' he offered in a friendly manner.

'No.'

The negative whipped loudly off her tongue and a wary alertness replaced the warmth in his eyes.

'Not breakfast or anything else, Mr Hunter,' Jo said very distinctly. 'I've changed my mind. I'm sorry you've been inconvenienced by coming here to pick me up, but it will only be wasting your time and mine to even continue this conversation.'

His face was stripped of good humour, his voice coldly implacable. 'Not my time, Jo, and I'll encroach on yours long enough for this change of mind to be discussed. Last night you agreed . . .'

'Last night I made an error of judgement. If you hadn't left the party so abruptly I would have told you so then. Now, I do apologise . . . .'

'What error?'

Her eyes flashed with impatience. 'Mr Hunter, I have nothing more to say to you.'

Jo began to close the door, but for the second time in the space of a few hours, she was brushed aside as the man pushed his way into her apartment. It was too much for Jo. She slammed the door shut and turned on him furiously, her blood fuming.

'Just who do you think you are, forcing your way into my home?'

He seemed to tower over her, an imposing presence which pulsed with hard purpose, yet his voice was deceptively soft when he spoke.

'It's not good manners to shut the door in a person's face, Jo, particularly in the face of a person who has every right to expect a polite reception. Now, you made a bargain with me last night, and I won't go until you give me your explanation for reneging on that bargain. I've been up since dawn this morning, working on the boat to have it ready in time to give you the pleasure of going sailing, and you haven't even done me the courtesy of being dressed in time for our appointment.'

A stab of guilt accompanied the hot flush which scorched her cheeks. Her hands moved instinctively to finger the edges of her housecoat, ensuring that she was decently covered. 'I didn't invite you in,' she defended hotly.

'I know,' he nodded, his expression remaining impassive. 'I invited you out, and I'm waiting to hear why you've changed your mind so capriciously. I thought you were a woman of your word, Jo, a woman who prided herself on her integrity.'

'How dare you throw *integrity* in my face!' she snapped. 'Don't you think I'm awake to your little game, Michael Hunter? Let me tell you, you've slipped up in your role as the puppetmaster. You don't have me on a string.'

He frowned, apparently puzzled by her assertion.

'What game?' he asked.

'Oh, stop pretending!' Jo demanded scornfully. 'Your contempt for people sickens me! You pretend one thing and do another.'

'I've never seen any merit in pretending anything. I can't recall one instance of having done what you claim. Would you please enlighten me?'

Jo's lip curled in derision. 'You hypocrite! Why bother bluffing it out? Don't you like having your game spoiled? Does it hurt your ego that you can't fool this particular woman when all other women grovel at your feet begging to be noticed?'

'You're evading the question,' Michael said tightly.

She noted that his pose had lost its indolence, as if his body had tensed along with his voice.

'Did you think Peg McAlister would keep her mouth shut?' she tossed at him. 'Why, she couldn't wait to pour it all out, how you hurried over and very single-mindedly separated me from Mark. She had this quaint idea that you were passionately interested in me, but of course she didn't know the background, couldn't possibly guess at the devious game you were playing!'

His very stillness had a threatening quality. 'So what do you think, Jo?' he asked quietly.

'I think you're a clever manipulator, Michael Hunter. You even had me fooled for a while, but the experience only confirmed what I knew all along. Nothing you say can be trusted.'

'I see. And that's what you think of me.'

'Yes, that's what I think of you,' she repeated contemptuously.

'You couldn't be more wrong—but then you don't

have much perception of people, do you, Jo? You didn't even know your own sister.' He straightened up and his eyes were bleak with disillusionment. 'You did make an error of judgement last night, but not the one you imagined. It would have been a simple matter to warn Mark off you if I'd thought it necessary. But I made a worse error.'

He sighed and walked slowly over to where she stood, just inside the door. He raised one hand and lightly brushed her cheek in a mocking kind of salute and farewell. She flinched and he gave her a sadly wry smile.

'I thought that underneath the veneer of sophistication you hadn't changed, but you have. I thought I could reach the girl I once met, but she's become hard and cynical and twisted beyond recognition. I don't want to spend the day with the present Jo Standish. Please forgive me for wasting your time.'

He nodded politely and reached past her for the doorknob. Jo felt ravaged by his words, torn in too many ways to put her thoughts together. Her empty stomach battled with sudden nausea and her heart ached with the weight of tormenting doubts. Michael had already opened the door when she turned to him, compelled by a blind sense of urgency.

'Wait!'

He had paused before she spoke. His hand was reaching for Mark's watch, still lying on the table. He picked it up, almost in slow motion, staring at it for a long moment, then he turned, his eyes slicing through her housecoat and examining her as if she was so much unwholesome meat. His mouth curled in distaste and his voice cut like a scalpel.

'I was wrong about a lot of things, wasn't I? I'll return this to Mark. He should be told the truth about the woman he's getting involved with.'

The blood drained from Jo's face as the full impact of his words hit her. She tried to speak, but the door was already closing behind him and she watched it click shut with a dull sense of resignation. What did it matter what he thought? she asked herself stubbornly. He was gone, and there was no reason for her to feel so bereft, so cut by his opinion of her. It did not matter.

She wandered disconsolately into the kitchen and filled the percolater. She needed a cup of coffee, something to settle her stomach, to take away the sick, hollow feeling. Nothing had gone the way she had expected, but at least she had her wish. Her personal life was free of the Hunters. Neither man would bother her again, but she had not come out of either encounter with any credit. Surely that was why she was feeling so miserable.

She had been a bitch to Mark. Whatever his shortcomings of character she had demeaned herself by leading him on. And Michael. Had he really been sincere? She remembered the warm glow in his eyes as he said, 'You're the woman of my choice.' She was not his choice any more. Her pride had fixed that, her pride and Mark's watch. She ground her teeth in frustration. How could he have thought she would take Mark as a lover? The way he had looked at her made her skin crawl even now.

Her eyes blurred with tears and her heart held a nameless ache. If only she had believed him! If only . . . She pulled herself up, shocked at the way she was thinking. Hard and cynical and twisted, he had called her, and if that was true, then it was Michael Hunter who had made her that way, he and his cousin. She was well rid of them. Well rid of them, she kept repeating determinedly.

CHAPTER EIGHT

'DID you remember to bring your lunch with you, Miss Standish?' Neville McKay greeted her, holding up a pack of cards as a reminder.

'Yes, of course,' she smiled, relieved to be back in the ordinary atmosphere of work. The weekend had been shadowed by too much mental agonising. She glanced across at Ian Cornish, who was reddening with embarrassment. 'Have you played much Bridge, Mr Cornish?'

'A few years,' he mumbled.

'What bidding system do you use?'

'Precision mostly, but I can play others.'

She nodded. 'Precision suits me. We'll give Mr McKay and Mr Barrington a run for their money.'

They hooted in confident derision, but there was a smile of quiet pleasure on Ian Cornish's face. Knowing how accurate he tried to be in his work, Jo felt sure that his card game would be equally accurate. She looked forward to the lunchtime duel between the two partnerships.

Elsie came bustling in at the morning tea break.

' 'Ave a good weekend, luv?' she asked with her customary cheerfulness.

'Not really,' Jo replied with a telling grimace.

Elsie gave a deflated sigh as she put Jo's cup on the desk. 'Seems as if everyone's got Monday mornin' blues. Not a smile anywhere!'

Jo smiled an apology. 'I guess I am a bit mopey this morning.'

'Well, at least yer not as glum as them upstairs. Yer would've thought Mr Michael an' Mr Mark were attendin' a funeral, their faces were so long.'

Probably Carol's funeral, Jo thought bitterly. Michael Hunter would not have held anything back from Mark. She wondered what Mark had told him. It did not matter, she repeated stubbornly, and shrugged off the speculation. 'They probably have a business problem,' she remarked casually to Elsie.

'That'd be right, with Mr Michael goin' off to Brisbane,' Elsie nodded with ready agreement. 'Yer'll 'ave to be watchin' Mr Mark — 'e'll be throwin' 'is weight around.'

Jo gave her a thin smile. 'I doubt that I'll need to watch him.'

'Put 'im in 'is place, did yer?' Elsie asked with relish.

'I'm sure he's lost interest.'

'Don't bet on it, Miss Jo. 'E likes 'is own way,' was Elsie's warning as she waddled out.

But Mark did not come anywhere near Jo. She did not even see him from a distance. The lunchtime card game became a regular routine and the competition was keen between the two partnerships. Formality quickly disappeared as Jo became more familiar with the programmers, and she enjoyed their easy friendship.

On Friday afternoon Bob Anderson dropped into her office for a review of the week's work. Jo was glad for an excuse to rest. Her whole body seemed to be aching, and she could not think why. It was not as if she had done any strenuous exercising. She sat back listlessly as Bob settled himself.

'You look a bit washed out, Jo. Tough week?'

'No, it went well, actually. Everything's on schedule. I just feel rotten. Must be coming down with something.'

'Don't get sick, for God's sake,' he said unsympathetically. 'I can't carry your load. I've got enough on my plate getting my own men up to scratch.'

'I won't get sick. I'm a big, healthy girl,' she assured him with a weak grin.

'So I've noticed,' he retorted dryly. 'I see you've got a card game going with your programmers.'

'Not me. I was invited.'

'Well, remember me if you're short a player,' he sighed. 'I'd enjoy the odd game now and then. A bit of relaxation between hassles is what I need. Haven't seen much of Mark Hunter this week. What about you?'

'Hasn't been near me.'

Bob gave her a curious look and then shrugged. 'Well, we don't have to worry about him any more anyway. He's off home. Now, about next week . . . .' He outlined various problems and they discussed them in detail.

It was four-thirty by the time he left, and Jo decided to leave work early. She did not feel at all well. She was just reaching for her handbag when a light tap came to her door and Mark Hunter entered quickly, a grim set to his too-handsome face. Jo tensed.

'Is there anything I can do for you, Mr Hunter?' she asked in a coldly businesslike tone.

'May I sit down?' he asked on a slightly hesitant note.

Jo waved to the office chair. Even when he sat his

posture was oddly stiff and his eyes did not quite meet hers.

'I'm flying home tonight,' he began hurriedly. 'I doubt that I'll be up here again before you leave us.' He rubbed at his hands and when he raised his gaze again he looked directly at her. 'I want to apologise for my behaviour the other night.'

'There's no need,' Jo said abruptly, discomfited by the concern in his eyes.

He winced and raked fingers through his curly hair. 'When I think of how you must have felt last week when I . . . I am sorry, Jo. You must have found me very offensive. If Mike had told me!' He shook his head. 'I didn't know about your sister's death or how it happened.'

'Please,' Jo broke in harshly, 'I don't want to discuss it. We really don't have anything to say to each other except goodbye. I wish we'd never said hello,' she added dispiritedly.

He nodded and stood up but was reluctant to go. 'I never meant to hurt Carol, you know.'

'I know,' Jo sighed. 'To you she was just another girl who gave freely of her favours. I'm sure your persuasion was masterly. Goodbye, Mark.'

'I don't expect you to believe me, but there was no need of persuasion, Jo. I didn't seduce Carol. She . . . .'

'Goodbye, Mark.' Jo bit the words out, her eyes flaring a warning.

He made a hopeless little gesture. 'There's no defence for me when she's dead, is there? Goodbye, Jo.'

She watched him go, then buried her face in her hands. Mark's visit had made her feel worse. She had to get home. Her legs felt like jelly when she stood up, but she forced them to work. Attacks of dizziness made the trip home a nightmare, but she made it.

Having swallowed some aspirin she crawled into bed, hoping to sleep off her ailment. Severe cramps wakened her in the middle of the night, and she just made it to the bathroom before retching violently. Her skin was clammy with fever and the convulsive shivering would not stop. She took some more aspirin and staggered back to bed.

By morning pain accompanied any movement. If she tried to get up she immediately felt faint, her body shaking uncontrollably and her head whirling in dark circles. Jo could not remember ever having felt so ill. Supporting herself against walls and furniture, she lurched into the living-room and telephoned her doctor.

He listened to her symptoms, assured her that he would call and suggested it was probably the virus which was commonly attacking a lot of his patients. Jo unlocked her front door ready for him and made her way back to bed in fits and starts, the now familiar giddiness making the journey hazardous.

Time dragged on and she was dozing fitfully when the doctor arrived. He quickly confirmed his diagnosis, told her to stay in bed for at least three days and gave her some capsules which would alleviate the symptoms. He was about to leave when the doorbell rang.

'Ah, good! You've got someone coming in to look after you.'

'No—I don't know who,' Jo said weakly. 'Please send them away.'

'Pity!' he nodded. 'You could do with someone here. Still, just don't try to do too much too soon. You're sick and the illness will run its course. Stay in bed. Okay?'

'Yes. Thank you, Doctor.'

The doorbell rang again. Probably someone collecting for an appeal or charity, Jo thought as she heard the doctor open the door. The buzzing stopped abruptly and there was a low murmur of voices. The door shut and Jo closed her eyes. If she lay very still the pain was not so bad.

'Jo?'

She could not focus immediately. Dots danced in front of her eyes, but there was no mistaking that powerful physique, nor the deep timbre of the voice.

'Mind if I come in?'

'What . . . what are you doing here?' she forced out tiredly. She could not cope with Michael Hunter today.

He ignored her question, picked up the chair from near her dressing-table and drew it up to her bedside. 'I met the doctor at the door and he told me how ill you are. What can I do for you?'

'Please . . . go away. I can't . . . can't . . . .' She swallowed convulsively to moisten her dry throat, but the effort required to fight Michael Hunter was too much for her weakened state. Tears filled her eyes and in automatic defence she turned her head away from him. Pain stabbed through her temples at the sudden movement and a moan escaped her lips. Her fingers clutched agitatedly at the bedclothes in an instinctive grab for protection, but a large, warm hand covered one of hers and the movement was gently stilled.

'You need someone, Jo, and I'm here,' he said with soft concern.

'No!' she cried fretfully.

'Don't talk. The doctor said quiet rest. I'll stay and look after you.'

Very slowly, conscious of the threatening pain, she turned enough to be able to see him. With her free hand she pushed the damp hair away from her clammy forehead. Feverish green eyes searched the rugged-handsome face, finding only a puzzling, careworn expression.

'Why?' she croaked out.

'Because I want to,' he answered enigmatically.

It made no sense, no sense at all. What was he doing here, holding her hand as if he cared for her? Last week he had walked away, despising her. She frowned and pulled ineffectually at his hold. Her eyes appealed against the confusion he was wreaking.

'Why . . . why did you come? I thought . . . last week . . . I thought . . . .'

He sighed and leaned forward, tenderly smoothing the anxious lines from her forehead. His voice was a deep rumble, a harsh note of stress creeping through. 'Don't talk, Jo. Just accept that I'm here. I don't want to cause you pain.'

'No—please tell me. I can't accept. How can I?' she whispered, an agony of uncertainty in the hoarse words.

The soft caress was withdrawn. He bent his head, heavy lids shielding his eyes from the limpid vulnerability in hers. The silence was fraught with tension. Her fingers fluttered nervously and his hold on them tightened as at last he raised a face which revealed all too clearly an inward struggle. The tanned skin looked sallow, stretched tightly over a clenched jaw-line, and the blue eyes mirrored the uncertainty in hers.

'I came because I had to find out if I was wrong.'

The words were flat and unemotional, yet there was no lack of emotion in his eyes. Jo stared at him, not quite believing his words and wanting to refute what they meant. He could not really care about her, there had to be some other motive. But what? Her head throbbed, pounding with doubts and sus-picions, fighting a losing battle against the stark sincerity etched on his face.

'I can't . . . let you . . . no, don't,' she whispered, struggling to push forward a defence because he was attacking her in a new and frightening way and she felt so defenceless. She closed her eyes, shutting out that blue blaze of need which had fired an answering need within herself. The conflicting emotions he stirred were creating havoc. Her pulse was leaping erratically and she was too weak to gain any control. Her head was swimming and there was no strength to fight him. She slipped into unconsciousness, in-stinctively welcoming the merciful blankness.

It was a heavy, drugged sleep and she came out of it slowly, floating up like a diver from the depths, pausing as if to gather strength for the next level. Near the surface of awareness she lingered a while, subconsciously resisting that last stroke to complete wakefulness. Michael Hunter's image imprinted it-self on her mind, hazily at first, like part of a dream, but some nagging sense of reality persisted in telling her it was not a dream. Then sudden memory jolted her into alertness. Her eyelids flicked open and he

was there, sitting at her bedside, his attention fixed
on a magazine.

Shock sent waves of dizziness through her head.
She quickly closed her eyes, willing the nauseous fog
to clear. She had to think. Slowly she pieced together
the earlier scene with him, remembering his concern,
the strange admission that he had come to find out if
he was wrong and his need to know which had been
so intensely conveyed in his eyes. Did he really care
so much, or had that forceful impression only been a
fevered product of her imagination? But he was here,
she reasoned obscurely.

She lifted her heavy lashes a little and studied him
intently. It was so strange to find him here, in her
bedroom, the man she had hated so much, here,
offering to look after her. It gave her an odd, shifting
feeling, as if the firm ground of her hatred was
dissolving into quicksand. She remembered Mark's
apology yesterday. It had been unexpected, surprising in his sensitive understanding of her reactions to
him, not like the callous Mark she had envisaged at
all. Yesterday she had been too distracted by her
physical malaise to give it consideration, but now, if
she had misjudged Mark, what of Michael? She felt
disturbingly confused.

He glanced up from his magazine and caught her
narrowed scrutiny. 'Have you been awake long?' he
asked softly.

Jo tried to speak, but her mouth was dry and her
lips felt swollen. Her tongue licked out trying to
moisten them. Michael moved quickly to pick up a
jug of water from her bedside table and pour out a
glassful, and she struggled to raise herself.

'Wait—I'll help you.'

Then a strong, supporting arm was around her shoulders, lifting her slightly while pillows were propped behind. He lowered her gently on to them and passed her the glass of water. Jo sipped slowly, letting the water roll around her hot mouth before swallowing carefully.

'You've slept almost four hours. Should you take more of these capsules now?'

She nodded and held up two fingers. He tapped them out of the vial and handed them to her. They were awkward to swallow, but she gulped them down. Her head was not aching quite so badly now, but the rest of her had not improved.

'Thanks,' she murmured, handing him back the glass.

'Want to lie down again?'

'No.' She held up a hand, ready to fend off his help. Embarrassing though the situation was, she had to go to the bathroom. 'Would you . . . please . . . find my housecoat in the wardrobe. I have to get up.'

Although her cotton nightie was not exactly transparent, it was thin enough to reveal too much to Michael Hunter's view. He brought the housecoat to her and held it so that she could easily slip her arms into it.

'I can manage,' she protested weakly, but he ignored her.

Satisfied that she was decently covered, Jo slid her legs over the side of the bed and stood up. The effort was a disaster. She swayed and clutched frantically at the bedside table for support, knocking the jug of water over.

'Oh God!' she sobbed, and before she could recover her balance, Michael had scooped her up and was cradling her comfortably in his arms.

'The bathroom?' he asked gently.

'Yes,' she whispered, tears of frustration gushing into her eyes.

She was held firmly against his broad chest and carried out of the bedroom, along the hallway and into the bathroom. Then he carefully set her on her feet, even placing her hand on the towel-rail for temporary support.

'Call me when you're ready. I'll wipe up the water and change your sheets.'

'Thank you,' she said shakily, unable to look up at him, so confused was she by his very physical help.

She took her time. She felt fresher for the wash, but found it too much of an effort to run a comb through her tangled hair. Her appearance did not matter anyway, she decided despondently. If Michael Hunter wanted to be here, then he could just accept her as she was. Determined not to be dependent on him, Jo made a rocky trip back to the bedroom, leaning on the wall to keep herself upright. Her bed was stripped but for a clean bottom sheet, and Michael was replacing fresh-looking pillows against the bedhead when she staggered through the doorway.

'Damn!' he muttered, moving quickly to her side as she tottered towards the bed.

'I can make it,' she said irritably.

'Proud and stubborn,' he declared just as irritably, putting a supporting arm around her shoulders. 'At least the bed's ready.' His fingers started loosening the tie-belt of her housecoat.

'No!' she cried, grabbing at it.

'For God's sake! You wouldn't have bothered with it if I wasn't here. Now you're not going to wear it to

bed. Have some sense, Jo. You're sick. I'm not going
to attack you, and you'll be uncomfortable in it.' All
the time he spoke he was insistently disrobing her.
'Now, into bed and I'll throw the top sheet over you.'

Jo obeyed because there was no other choice. It
was even pleasant to lay her flushed cheeks on cool,
clean linen. The top sheet was spread over her and
straightened, the corners tucked under in a very
professional manner.

'Thank you,' she muttered, totally embarrassed
now.

He looked down at her, hands on hips in a slightly
exasperated pose. 'Jo, I have at times nursed three
younger sisters, so this is nothing new to me. You're
too damned ill to be stiffnecked about accepting
help, so just give in and let me be useful.'

'I'm not used to . . . to accepting help,' she said,
half in apology, half in explanation.

'That I can believe,' he sighed, relaxing onto his
chair again. 'Do you ever let anyone near you, Jo?'

Her eyes flashed resentment. 'I had a sister once.'

He shook his head and sadness deepened the
sympathy in his eyes. 'I know you had a sister once,
Jo, but you weren't close. You were two entirely different people. You might have lived under the same
roof, but you lived separate lives. Isn't that true?'

She hesitated, reluctant to agree with him even
though it was true. He plunged on without waiting
for an answer.

'You were a serious student and your sister was a
social butterfly. There was no similarity in personality or character. Your only meeting point was the
fact that you were family. I'm right, aren't I?'

'In a way,' she admitted slowly. 'Carol was an

extrovert, outgoing and very popular. I was . . . I still
am an introvert, I suppose. Carol always used to say
I hid behind books. I hid too well that year. Maybe
if . . . .'

'No,' he interrupted purposefully, 'don't start on
the "if onlys", Jo. Carol was leading her own life and
she was responsible for herself and whatever she did.
Every adult person is responsible for the choices he
or she makes.'

'Adult? She was only eighteen!' Jo insisted, sitting
up to make the point more vehemently. Her head
whirled and she clutched at it to steady the sickening
circles.

He gave a defeated sigh. 'I hurt you very badly,
didn't I, Jo?'

She licked her lips which were suddenly very dry.
'Why do you say that?' she asked, unwilling to let
him know how deeply the hurt had gone.

'Only an intense personal hurt produces such
determined hatred.'

His statement demanded an answer. It probed the
old wound, re-opening the agony of his betrayal of
trust, dragging out the core of pain. 'I was . . .
counting on . . . your help.'

She was unaware of the terrible vulnerability in
her eyes as she spoke. The poignant memory of
betrayal was mirrored there, causing him to wince
and draw in a sharp breath.

'Oh God!' he groaned, and covered his eyes with
one hand. He rubbed tiredly at the lids before dragging the hand slowly down his face, finally dropping
it to his lap. He then raised both hands in a hopeless
gesture of appeal. 'What can I say to that? How do
you wipe away pain?'

His hands slapped down on his thighs and he stood up and paced away from her, clearly too agitated to remain still. Jo stared after him, deeply moved by the anguish he had shown. For her. It had been anguish for the pain he had caused *her*. The thought was stunning, a revelation which tapped inexorably at her repressed feeling for him.

'Jo, that first night we met . . . when you came for Mark's address.' The words burst from him as he paused in his stride. Then he turned to face her, his whole body taut with urgency. ' . . . Before everything got twisted up in my mind . . . you were someone with whom I felt a sense of accord, someone I felt . . . .'

His hand lifted and clenched into a fist. His jaw jutted out angrily and his next words were explosive with pent-up feeling. 'Dammit—I let you go! I not only let you go, I turned you completely against me. Three years! Three years, and you walk back into my life with hatred, hostility, bitter rejection . . . and yet . . . .' He paused, his eyes searching hers. 'Yet I have the same feeling about you, as if . . . if only I can reach past those barriers between us, then . . . .'

He drew in a deep breath and shook his head in puzzlement. 'Then last Sunday I thought I'd been fooling myself—but, Jo, I can't quite believe you've changed so much. Last Sunday was all wrong. It had to be wrong, because I felt it so strongly at the party when we were talking, a deep sense of accord, like an inner recognition of kinship. It was only fleeting because you guard yourself well, but it was there.' His eyes burned down at her, scorching into her soul. 'Tell me I'm right.'

Her lashes flicked down, veiling the response

which leapt from her heart. Her brain dictated caution. She fixed her gaze on her fingers which slowly gathered pleats into the top sheet, measuring out the material with deliberate care. 'Supposing . . .' she began and paused, apprehensive about surrendering the truth. 'Supposing I said you were right . . . tell me how I could trust such a feeling?'

For a big man he moved surprisingly fast. The instant after she had spoken he was back on the bedside chair and her hand was captured in both of his.

'Jo, I swear to you that I'll never knowingly hurt you again. I can't wipe out the past, but that was Mark and Carol involving us in an affair which wasn't ours. A chance was lost then, but this is another chance, and I think it's possible that we could share something important together. I know it's asking a great deal for you to push the past aside, but, Jo, couldn't we start afresh, just you and me, getting to know each other? Couldn't we try it and see where it leads us?'

Jo fought off the surge of emotion which begged her to say yes. That was blind unreason. 'I'm . . . I'm not sure,' she said uncertainly.

'Not even for a little while, Jo? To see if you could learn to trust me again?' he pleaded softly.

She wrenched her eyes away from him. Her heart was pounding with a crazy life of its own, creating havoc in her veins. She spoke fast, her breath almost panting in her agitation. 'The past is too much part of me. You don't understand. What happened back then . . . it changed my life, shattered it in so many ways I couldn't begin to tell you. And you . . . you're part of it, twisted into the fabric. It's impossible to extricate those threads.'

'Then we'll work another tapestry on top of them, blotting them out.'

The words were soft but intensely determined. Jo looked back at him, an agony of doubt written on her face. 'You don't know what you're asking.'

Michael paused and then admitted slowly, 'No, I probably don't. I don't know you well enough, Jo. I think you're afraid of letting yourself be vulnerable, especially to me, but I'm not asking you to let down your guard. I'm asking for a truce to begin with. If you can put the hostility aside and just let us talk openly and honestly to each other, it would give us some foundation to build on. Does that seem so impossible?'

'No . . . I suppose not,' she answered hesitantly.

He relaxed and the pressure on her hand eased. He looked down, as if only now becoming conscious of having it in his possession. A faint smile curved his lips as he fondled it gently. 'I'll play safe and ask about your health. In fact, if I'd been thinking along a business line, I should have asked how long you've been ill. For all I know the programming department might be in chaos.'

'No,' she assured him, a smile tugging at her own lips. 'I was off colour all yesterday, but I worked. This bug didn't really hit me until last night.'

'Well, the doctor says you're not to get up for at least two days, and I'm telling you you're not to come back to work until you're completely better. Will the men manage on their own, or should I get someone in?'

Jo frowned, trying to think ahead. 'They'll manage. I'll phone Bob and Neville McKay.'

'McKay?'

'He's very good and a natural leader. He'll carry the responsibility.'

'You're sure?'

She smiled a faintly ironic smile. 'About that, yes. It won't be for long, and Bob will lend a hand if he needs it.'

'Have you always poured yourself into your work, Jo?' he asked curiously.

'I guess so,' she sighed. 'It gives me satisfaction, and a certain amount of confidence in myself. I know I'm good at it, you see.'

'Yes, Mark was very impressed with you.' He frowned and then added tentatively. 'It didn't occur to me that he would pursue you in a personal way, or I would have spoken to him. He was very upset when I did explain the situation.' He drew in a deep breath and expelled it slowly before continuing. 'And I have another apology to make to you. I thought . . . oh, God knows what I thought, but it was all wrong. Mark told me what happened between you. He felt wretched about it.'

'So it would seem,' Jo mused. 'He actually apologised yesterday. I couldn't quite take it in. My head was aching and it didn't fit . . . .'

'Didn't fit your image of him?' Michael shook his head. 'He's not the type of person you've assumed him to be, Jo. In fact, the woman he married carved him up into little pieces and he puts on a brashness to cover his insecurity, particularly with women.'

'I shouldn't have gone out with him,' Jo muttered, and looked away, ashamed of her motives. 'He made me so mad I thought I'd teach him a lesson, but I'm no good at pretending, and I hated the party. I just wanted it to end so I could get away from him.'

'And me,' he prompted gently.

'Yes,' she admitted with a sigh. 'I didn't want to see you again. It made me feel sick to think I'd let myself be fooled.'

'I wasn't fooling, Jo.'

She wrinkled her nose at him. 'You did start off with "You look beautiful tonight", or some such glib phrase.'

He grinned in reminiscence. 'For which you promptly took me to task. I was only speaking the truth.'

'Well, as you can plainly see today, I'm not beautiful, and even though the tricks I was taught have proved useful . . . .' She gave him a wry look. 'I know it's only cosmetics, not me at all.'

An amused twinkle brightened his eyes. 'But cosmetics only enhance what you have, and you're beautiful, Jo. Why should you think anyone pitied you?'

'Oh, come on,' she replied derisively. 'I was a great big lump of a girl, and you know it. No one ever asked me for a date until after I got myself remodelled.'

Michael shook his head bemusedly. 'I don't remember you like that. You weren't so slim or elegantly polished as you are now, but you had a proud beauty which was unforgettable.'

'Then you were the only one who ever thought so,' she scoffed, but the compliment pleased her enormously.

'Maybe you only lacked confidence in yourself and the remodelling gave it to you,' he suggested.

'Oh, I don't know,' she sighed. 'It did in a way, but when it comes right down to it, I intimidate most men—too tall and too intelligent. It's a hell of a combination!'

'Not for me. I like it.'

She looked at him wonderingly. 'This is crazy! The fever must have touched my brain. Here I am, telling you things I've never told anybody.'

He smiled encouragement. 'I like that too. Please don't stop, unless you feel tired. Rest when you want to, but I'd enjoy nothing better than talking to you all weekend.'

And they did, in between periods of restful sleep. It was a strangely intimate weekend. Michael fussed over her, fetching her drinks, tempting an appetite with carefully prepared food, helping her to the bathroom, even brushing her hair. And they talked at great length, each of them greedy to learn as much as possible about the other.

Their conversation roamed over many subjects, finding common interests in their enjoyment of books and music and the theatre. They discussed their time at university, Michael revealing that he had majored in Maths at Monash University in Melbourne. His family lived in Melbourne, and with his training in statistics, he had first joined his father's market research company down there. His ambition to run his own business had brought him to Sydney eight years ago. Oddly enough, Elsie had been his mother's cleaning lady. She had come to Sydney at the same time to live with a newly widowed daughter and Michael had offered her the job of tea-lady, knowing she wanted a bit of independence and was getting too old for rigorous cleaning jobs.

Jo made little protest when he insisted on staying

the night. She warned him he would be uncomfortable, but he slept on the foldaway bed in the spare
room and was on hand as soon as she stirred in the
morning. By Sunday night they were completely
comfortable in each other's company, and Jo was
reluctant to see him go. Physically she felt a great
deal better but was still weak and shaky on her legs.

'I'll come around after work tomorrow and cook
you a proper meal,' Michael promised her. 'You
should feel up to it by then.'

'You're spoiling me,' she smiled.

'That's my pleasure,' he grinned, then bent over
and brushed her forehead with a light kiss. 'Now,
take good care of yourself until I get back to you.'

The flush on her face had nothing to do with
illness. 'I will,' she assured him, and he left her with
the warm glow on her face spreading through her
body.

CHAPTER NINE

AT eleven o'clock the next morning a large sheaf of yellow roses was delivered to her apartment. The card read, 'To make you smile and feel better. Mike.' She needed no prompting to smile. The roses were beautiful and their scent seemed to fill the apartment.

At four o'clock he telephoned to ask how she was and if there was anything she wanted which he could bring with him. His kind consideration warmed her heart, and her eyes glowed with happiness as later she watched him lightheartedly prepare a meal in her kitchen. He insisted on treating her as an invalid, propping her up with cushions on one of the chesterfield lounges and not letting her lift a finger except to eat and drink.

The hours flew past, and again Jo was reluctant to see him go. It was the same on Tuesday night, but he did allow her to help with the meal. She was almost well again and although she suggested she return to work the next day, Mike insisted she stay at home and not over-exert herself too soon.

Jo felt restless on Wednesday. Her illness had cooped her up inside for too long and she felt reasonably well. On impulse she went out shopping, deciding she would surprise Mike by having a meal prepared for him tonight. The smell of a chicken casserole alerted him to her activities as soon as he arrived. He shook his head at her in reproval.

'I thought I told you . . . .'

'But I'm better, really I am,' she protested quickly. 'In fact I felt a real fraud staying at home today.'

'Eight hours in an office is more taxing than a few jobs at home,' he retorted, 'but I'm glad to see you properly on your feet. I've bought tickets for the new play at the Royal. Do you think you'll feel up to it by Friday night?'

'I surely will.' She smiled happily at him. 'Thanks, Mike. You've been wonderful to me.'

Then slowly and very gently he drew her into his arms. For a long moment he just held her against him as if savouring the feel of her body. His eyes caressed her face, seeing the soft compliance in her expression. 'It's very easy to be wonderful to you, Jo,' he murmured.

She knew he was going to kiss her, and wanted him to. His mouth descended on hers and she surrendered her lips willingly. Her hands crept around his neck and she pressed closer, eagerly exploring the sensations he was arousing. The kiss began as a sweet tasting, but grew in fervour with her wholehearted response. It was a beautiful kiss, a long, lingering kiss which stirred her innate sensuality and awakened a desire for more intimacy. It stopped short of real passion, and she felt Mike's touch on her cheek, a feather-light touch that made her skin tingle. She sighed and opened her eyes. He smiled down at her and she knew the glow of satisfaction in his eyes was mirrored in hers.

'I've wanted to do that for a long time, and it was everything I ever wished,' he said softly.

Jo blushed and looked down, very conscious of her

galloping pulse. She slid her hands down to his tie and fiddled with it distractedly. 'I wanted it too,' she whispered huskily, 'but, Mike . . . .' She hesitated, not quite sure how to put her feeling into words.

'You don't want to be rushed,' he finished for her with wry tenderness. 'I understand, Jo. It's still too new for you, isn't it?'

She nodded, grateful for his understanding.

'I can wait until you're sure.' He tilted her chin upwards, giving her a warm look of reassurance. 'I'm a very patient man when I know patience is worthwhile. Now, perhaps we'd better have this meal you've cooked.'

'Yes,' she agreed quickly.

He laughed. It was a laugh of pure happiness and it set the atmosphere for the evening. There was a deep joy in every word and gesture, and when he finally took his leave with only a light, teasing kiss, Jo was almost certain she was in love with him. It just seemed too incredible that one could fall in love on such short acquaintance. Only time could define her feelings more assuredly, but she went to bed very contented with their relationship.

She went back to work the next morning to find that everything had proceeded smoothly in her absence, even the lunchtime card game. Bob had partnered Ian Cornish, who promptly remarked that he was more comfortable with her as a partner. Bob Anderson took too many risks. Jo laughed and promised to be extra cautious in future. Her own work programme was slightly behind, so she concentrated hard on getting it up to date, allowing only a few necessary interruptions from the men. Only Elsie had the temerity to insist that she take it easy.

'Yer need someone to look after yer,' she said knowingly.

'Maybe I'll get someone,' Jo grinned.

'Someone nice and solid like Mr Michael,' Elsie hinted broadly.

Jo got the strong impression that Elsie more than suspected an involvement between them and her next words confirmed it. 'Don't think I can't see, Miss Jo. That Suzie Trigg's turnin' green about some phone calls Mr Michael's been makin', so yer better watch out. She's a nasty piece of work where 'e's concerned.'

It annoyed Jo to think that Mike's secretary had listened in on private conversations. It annoyed her even further when Susan Trigg caught up with her on her way to Wynyard Station that afternoon.

'I see you're quite well again, Miss Standish,' she said sweetly.

'Yes, thank you.'

'Were the yellow roses to your taste?'

Jo faltered in her step, glancing sharply at the smug smile on Susan Trigg's face.

'I thought yellow would suit you. Mr Hunter never sends red ones, you know,' she continued nonchalantly. 'Occasionally he specifies a colour, but it's never red. I must say he's very generous with his women—but then they never last long.'

Jo kept walking, ignoring the sly dig. Not having drawn blood, Susan Trigg tried another thrust.

'He usually finishes them off with white carnations. It's funny, I always think of white carnations as wedding flowers, but I guess they're used at funerals too. Anyhow, it's easy to tell when an affair is dead. White carnations every time. I cross over here for my bus stop. I'm glad you're feeling better, Miss Standish. 'Bye now.'

The poisonous little darts had momentarily pricked Jo, but Elsie's warning had echoed in her ear. Susan Trigg was a nasty piece of work. As for her assertions, Jo decided to ignore them. She was not going to let Susan Trigg cast a shadow on her relationship with Mike. It was already important to her and it promised far too much for any casual spite to affect it.

She hugged a smile to herself. Although he was not coming around to her apartment tonight, having suggested she would need a good rest after returning to work, tomorrow night was an exciting prospect to look forward to. She would enjoy the play in Mike's company and they would have supper afterwards and it would all be marvellous.

Her pleasurable anticipation was considerably heightened by the time she was dressed and ready for him on Friday night. Her eyes sparkled with happiness as she surveyed herself in the mirror. Mike could not say she needed rest tonight. He had seen her at her worst last weekend. Tonight she had made a special effort to look her best. Her hair had co-operated fully with her skilful hands, her make-up was masterly and the green silk dress clung lovingly to every curve. When she opened the door to him the look in Mike's eyes curled her nerve-ends into knots.

He expelled a long breath and gave her a slightly wry look. 'Am I allowed to say you look beautiful tonight?'

'Yes,' she replied laughingly.

'Then you do indeed look beautiful,' he murmured, drawing her into his arms.

'Thank you. I wanted you to be proud of me,' she explained shyly.

'Jo, I'd be proud of you in rags, but I appreciate the effort,' he replied, his eyes gently teasing her.

She wrinkled her nose at him. 'Well, you did see me at my worst last weekend, and you are taking me out in public.'

Mike raised one eyebrow and muttered darkly, 'I think I'd prefer us to stay at home. To hell with the tickets!'

She linked her hands behind his head and smiled up at him. 'Oh, no, you don't, Mike Hunter!'

'You expect me to share you?'

'I expect you to take me to the theatre as you promised. I'm sick of the four walls of my apartment. I need a night out.' She also needed a breathing space. Mike looked devastatingly handsome in a dress suit, and she was acutely aware of her quickened response to him.

'If we must, we must,' he sighed resignedly, and led her out.

The theatre was packed. The play was living up to its critical acclaim. It was a clever, satirical comedy about political climbers, an apt social comment that was highly entertaining. Jo's pleasure in it was measurably increased by sharing it with Mike. Occasionally their eyes would meet in appreciation over a witty line and always there was the heady warmth of his close contact, his arm linked with hers, his strong fingers stroking her hand.

During the main interval they strolled out to the foyer. Mike left her near an archway while he manoeuvred his way to the bar, intent on buying drinks. Jo had no doubt he would manage to be served quickly. His imposing figure automatically commanded attention. He glanced back at her reassuringly and Jo suddenly felt that nothing else mattered but to be with this man.

Lost in her musing, she was not particularly aware of the people around her until becoming slowly conscious that someone was staring at her. The woman was a stunning redhead and she was startlingly familiar. Jo met her gaze curiously, trying to place where she had seen the woman before. There was an air of haughty hostility about her that was puzzling. Then Mike was back at her elbow offering her a glass of champagne.

'Thank you,' she smiled up at him, then nodded in the woman's direction. 'Mike, do you know the redhead in the black dress? I seem to recognise her, but. . . .'

'Eva Daniels. You've probably seen her on television. She's an actress,' he explained matter-of-factly.

'Of course! I wonder why she was looking at me. I don't know her,' Jo remarked innocently, and was surprised by the sudden change of expression on Mike's face.

An impervious mask seemed to settle on his features, his eyes narrowing into slits as he muttered, 'You're about to. She's coming over.'

Jo was rudely brushed aside as Eva Daniels insinuated herself next to Mike, a predatory hand clinging to his sleeve. 'Mike, darling,' she purred huskily. 'Fancy seeing you here!'

'Hello, Eva,' he said, coolly disentangling himself and drawing Jo back to his side. 'May I introduce Jo Standish—Jo, Eva Daniels.'

Jo smiled automatically, but Eva barely nodded in her direction.

'Why didn't you tell me you wanted to see this play, Mike? I could easily have got you tickets,' she complained prettily.

'I prefer to make my own arrangements, Eva,' he replied casually. 'That way there are no strings attached. You know I don't like being pinned down.'

'And of course there's always that business of yours interfering, isn't there?'

Jo could not mistake the acid in her voice as Eva Daniels turned to her.

'Are you a business acquaintance of Mike's, Miss Standish? Or is it Mrs?'

'No, on both counts,' Mike said quite firmly before Jo could open her mouth.

There was a venomous flash from Eva's eyes before she turned on an ultra-sweet smile. 'I see. I suppose you expect me to make a graceful exit.'

'I wouldn't like to see you lose your style, Eva,' Mike replied sardonically.

Her smile dropped for a moment, then tilted slyly. 'Ah yes, by all means let's have some style.' She turned to Jo, malice glinting in her eyes. 'I do hope you find his bed warmer than I did, my dear. He has a very cold habit of switching off his mind. Tata, darling.'

Mike muttered something under his breath, but Jo watched thoughtfully as Eva Daniels weaved her way through the crowd and disappeared from sight. The blunt statement had not really surprised her; the undercurrents had been quite plain during the short conversation.

'Jo!'

There was an anxious note in Mike's voice and she turned back to him.

'Didn't you send her white carnations, Mike?' It was a catty thing to say, and Jo was surprised at the swift stab of jealousy that had prompted her words.

'What?'

His frown was puzzled and Jo concluded that Susan Trigg had been lying in her teeth. She shrugged, pretending an indifference to the situation. 'Your secretary is rather indiscreet. She informed me that you begin an affair with roses and end it with white carnations.'

'The bitch!' Anger cut harsh lines on his face and his grip on her arm tightened. 'You didn't believe her, did you, Jo?'

'Not really. But your past affairs do seem to be rebounding around me at the moment,' she answered dryly.

'Pay no attention. Everything that's gone before is irrelevant. Only you and I matter—you know that, don't you, Jo?'

His eyes burned down at her, demanding confirmation. She hesitated, still a little shaken by the encounter with Eva Daniels. Then she nodded, accepting his insistence. The fire in his eyes subtly changed, reaching out and scorching her with hungry flames, kindling a dangerous flicker in her own veins. The warning bell jangled out, telling patrons to take their seats for the final act of the play, and the immediate bustle brought Jo down to earth.

'We'd better go in before the lights dim,' she suggested, and, a little dazed by her reaction, she started moving forward with the crowd.

The rest of the play was completely lost on Jo. A

feverish excitement was coursing through her, heating her blood until she was bubbling with inner exhilaration. 'I love him, I love him, I love him.' The words beat over and over in her brain like a drum-roll of anticipation. 'This is the man I've been waiting for all my life,' she thought in delighted wonder. She turned her head, irresistibly drawn to feast her eyes on him.

Almost instantly he returned her gaze, and she saw the leaping glow of triumph as he read the message of her eyes. He smiled and her heart turned over. She looked blindly back at the stage, conscious only of the hand entwining its fingers with hers, holding on with determined possession.

The final curtain came down at last. Jo automatically applauded and rose with the rest of the audience. Mike hurried her out, carving a relentless path through the crowd. His impatience communicated itself to her and they almost ran down the last few steps to the street outside. Not even the crisp night air cooled their blood.

'Home?' Mike demanded more than asked as he tucked her against him and began walking briskly to the car-park.

'Aren't you hungry?' she suggested mischievously.

He looked down at her with a deep, compelling hunger. 'Yes.'

Jo said nothing more. Words were stifled by the wild elation that surged through her. The need for privacy vibrated between them. Mike handed her into his car, and as he took the driver's seat, he sighed and sent her a look which expressed everything she felt herself.

'It's not a dream?'

She smiled reassurance. 'Maybe we should pinch ourselves.'

'I can think of something else I'd rather do, but not here.'

He started the motor and they drove to her apartment in a silence which carried blissful contentment. Once inside her living-room, Mike swept her into his arms, and Jo was caught up in a thunderous wave of desire.

All the hunger of years poured into their kiss, giving and taking with breathless abandon. She clung to him, her hands moving restlessly over his shoulders, her fingers burying themselves in the rough thickness of his hair, pressing, wildly encouraging the expression of a love that was consuming her. Mike was moulding her soft roundness to the hard length of his body with demanding pressure. It felt so right, so gloriously satisfying, and she willingly melted against him. When he finally dragged his mouth away from hers it was only to trail his lips down the curve of her throat. She shivered with delight, mesmerised by the sheer sensuality of his touch.

'Say you're mine, Jo,' he breathed into her ear.

'Yes,' she whispered huskily. 'I love you, Mike.'

'I'll love you as you've never been loved before, my darling,' he murmured, gently tilting her face back for his avid inspection. 'I can hardly believe it. Tell me it's true—that you're mine.'

'I'm yours,' she repeated, too drugged with love to think of saying anything else.

A sigh shuddered through him and then he was nestling her head against his throat as he rocked her in a fiercely possessive embrace. She breathed in the strong male scent of him, savouring his closeness.

His hand reached up and removed her hairpins. The chignon tumbled down and his fingers loosened the long tresses, tugging with impatience. Suddenly a laugh of sheer exultation bubbled up in him, and he lifted her into his arms and strode towards the bedroom.

'Tonight you're mine!'

It was a cry of triumph. Bedclothes were flung aside and Jo was gently laid on the cool sheet. His lips brushed against hers.

'No barriers, Jo—just you and me at last.'

She stared helplessly as he threw off his coat and tie and began removing his shoes. Things were moving too fast. Fear snaked through her, cooling her senses. She loved Mike, but as yet there had been no talk of marriage, and that was what a physical commitment meant to her. All the long-held inhibitions formed a protest, but before it could be spoken, Mike was warming her body with his own, stealing the words from her lips, kissing her until she was reeling from his ardour.

Slowly and with all the smooth skill of experience he began to remove her clothes, caressing her nakedness as it was revealed. Jo shivered, torn between the need to stop him and the wanton desire to let this madness continue.

'Mike!'

She moaned the name as his mouth freed hers, but every thought winged out of her mind as his lips travelled downwards, roaming over the swell of her breasts, his tongue tasting the changing texture of her skin as it explored the exposed peaks. Wave after wave of sensuality spread its intoxicating sweetness through her body.

Seemingly of their own volition her hands moved to explore, to touch, to know intimately. She pushed his shirt aside and thrilled to the feel of his skin against hers, the hair-roughened chest softly prickling. The last of her clothes were discarded without any thought of protest from her. She was too drugged with desire. She wanted Mike to possess her totally, be his for ever and ever.

'I've wanted you so much. You'll never know,' he murmured lovingly as he moved to strip off his own clothes.

Jo felt she was floating, strangely bereft without his touch. Then he lowered himself over her and she welcomed him back with a satisfied sigh. His lips moved across her forehead and softly closed her eyelids.

'Those eyes have looked at me in my dreams, always challenging me. You've obsessed my mind, Jo, and now at last it's true.' He pressed his cheek against hers, rubbing skin against skin in a worshipful kind of contact which was intensely moving. 'This time you won't go away. You're mine for as long as I want you.'

Even as his lips took hers in a final claim of ownership, those last words began working on her brain like corrosive acid. 'For as long as I want you,' a time-span built on his need, a need which might be quickly sated by a man of so much experience. A ripple of panic wavered uncertainly, then swelled as other words joined in force to build its momentum. Want, not love. 'I'll love you as you've never been loved before.' He had meant lovemaking, a physical act which had nothing to do with commitment. He wanted her, that was all. An obsession to have what had seemed impossible, a challenge taken up and won.

'No!' she moaned. Horror at the closeness of her surrender sparked a violent reaction. 'No, no, no!' she screamed, threshing wildly to escape from him.

'Jo, stop it!' he breathed raggedly. His greater weight frustrated her efforts, but she fought him, her mouth grimly set and her eyes begging frantically for freedom. 'What's wrong? What's wrong?' he repeated, his voice rough with urgency.

'Let me go!' she panted.

His voice softened into persuasion. 'Jo, this is crazy! You don't mean it. Let me love you as you want me to.'

'No—I won't let you!' she cried, desperation making her voice shrill.

'But you belong to me. We belong together. You know that—you said so.'

It was a cry from the soul, but Jo's ears were tuned elsewhere. Snatches of words were screeching through her mind, all the warning signals she had ignored. Peg, Mark, Eva, even Susan Trigg, they had all told her in various ways that Mike never belonged to any woman for long. Then like a dark shadow settling on her heart came the deeply etched memory of Carol, sobbing out her desperation when Mark had finished with her.

'No—never!' she groaned in despair. 'I'll never belong to you that way.'

'Why? For God's sake, why?'

Jo did not see the plea in his eyes. Her own were blinded by memory. 'You're just like Mark. But I'm not Carol and I never will be—not me. I'll never give in to you, Mike Hunter.'

'No!' It was a harshly indrawn breath and he shook his head. 'No, I won't let you do this, Jo. You're mine.'

Then his mouth plundered hers with a savagery that reduced her physical resistance to a limp rag. She called on her last reserve of strength, reaching back for the hatred she had once felt for him. She pried his head up and almost spat at him in her desperation.

'Taking's all you know, isn't it? The Hunter trademark! Taking what you want and leaving the rest to die. Remember my sister, Mike Hunter, and remember my hatred. Now let me go!'

Mike flung himself aside and lay there, one arm covering his face.

'Is there such a fine line between love and hatred?' he asked hoarsely.

She did not answer, frightened of revealing the turmoil jumbling around in her mind, the warring emotions which were tearing her apart.

His fingers dug remorselessly into her flesh. 'Is there, Jo?'

Stung into retaliation, she replied wildly, 'You and your cousin have no conception of love! The only word you know is want, and the Hunters have taken enough from the Standish family. You won't get me too!'

He released her and rolled away. 'So it all comes back to that,' he muttered in disgust. Then his voice sharpened with harsh accusation. 'Did you plan this all along, Jo? To make me believe and then plunge in the knife? A hurt for a hurt?'

The blood drained from her face as the implication of his words sliced through to her heart. He thought

she had deliberately led him up to this sordid rejection as a revenge for the past. The bitter irony of the
situation held her speechless. Then she realised it
was probably safer to let him keep believing it. If she
corrected him he might resume his efforts to persuade her into being his mistress, and she was still
too vulnerable to risk that.

With a weary sigh he reached for his clothes and
began to dress, taking her silence as confirmation. 'It
was a dangerous game to play, Jo,' he commented
dully. 'A man can get ugly under that kind of strain.
Funny—I never once considered it, that the hatred
would win. All I could see was you.'

He shuddered and stood up, and Jo looked away,
unable to bear the sight of his strong, virile body.
The memory of their intimacy shamed her. She
heard him walk towards the door and sighed with
relief, wanting only to be left alone to nurse her
wounded heart. The light flicked on, startling her
with its brightness. Mike turned towards her and she
shrank back instinctively. He had not bothered to do
up his shirt and his coat and tie were slung carelessly
over one shoulder. Grey, wintry eyes swept over her,
not missing any detail.

'You have nothing to fear from me, Jo,' he said
derisively. 'I don't want your hatred. We could have
had something good together, if you'd let us.'

She stared back at him with haunted eyes, disillu-
sion making her voice sharp. 'Good for you, you
mean? Another affair notched up?'

'Affair!' Mike rolled the word off his tongue with
stinging venom. 'Is that all you can think of? One
stupid, careless affair three years ago and it spawns
this . . . this virulent cancer of hatred in you. If I

could tear it out I would, but it's too deep-rooted, isn't it, poisoning your whole system. Are you satisfied now?'

'Satisfied?' she repeated blankly.

'With your pound of flesh. Has your appetite for revenge been satisfied, or are you after more blood? What's the next step, Jo? Are you after my business too? A little computer sabotage, perhaps?'

Tears welled up in her eyes and she was powerless to stop them. 'My only aim, Mike Hunter, is to get the job finished so I don't have to see you again,' she forced out through trembling lips.

'Tears,' he mocked. 'The woman's way to cover deceit! Well, at least you've put me on my guard, for which I should be thankful. You'd better be careful not to make one goddamned mistake at work, Jo, because I'll have you under a microscope. I won't risk any more to you. Goodnight!'

He snapped off the light and moments afterwards she heard the front door click shut. She crawled under the blankets and wound them around her. She felt cold right through to her bones, her whole body aching with a coldness which would not go away. A new chasm of loneliness yawned open and engulfed her, drawing her into a dark world of depression. She kept telling herself that there had been no other choice. No one, not even a man she loved, was going to use her as a casual bedmate. That would only shrivel her love to ashes anyway.

CHAPTER TEN

' 'ULLO! That virus playin' yer up again, Miss Jo? Yer don't look too good this mornin',' Elsie proclaimed as she placed Jo's coffee on her desk.

'I'm all right, thanks, Elsie,' she murmured, forcing a smile.

'Well,' Elsie sighed with gusto, 'it appears there's nothing right upstairs. Place is in an uproar.'

'Oh?'

'That Susan Trigg was given 'er walkin' papers and poor Linda Donnison from the typin' pool is standin' in, temporary like. She's scared stiff with Mr Michael lookin' like thunder. Everyone's jumpin' around like rabbits. Reckon they needed their coffee.'

'So do I,' Jo said feelingly.

'I bet that Susan Trigg stuck 'er nose in once too often. She's no loss, that's for sure,' Elsie nodded with satisfaction. 'Now don't work too 'ard, Miss Jo. Won't do yer no good gettin' sick again.'

'Whatever you say, Elsie,' Jo replied meekly.

'Well, yer should take notice,' Elsie grumbled goodnaturedly, and went on her way.

Hard work was exactly what she needed, Jo thought grimly. Anything that kept her from brooding over Mike Hunter was to be welcomed. The whole weekend had been utter misery, each lonely hour reminding her that it could have been different if she had not rejected him. Her brain told her she

154

had made the right choice, but her heart kept yearning for what could have been.

She wondered if Mike's frustration had triggered Susan Trigg's dismissal. The girl had been indiscreet, which was not an acceptable fault in a confidential secretary. As Elsie said, she was no loss to the Company. On the other hand, Jo felt uncomfortable about it. Up until last Friday Mike had probably been satisfied with Susan Trigg's work.

She suddenly realised that her thoughts were revolving around Mike again and she ruthlessly crushed her speculation. It was a fruitless exercise. She concentrated fiercely on her work, trying to block out any thought of him. The lunchtime card game gave her some relaxation. The friendly company of the other programmers inevitably drew her out of any private agonizing, and she was in a better frame of mind when Bob Anderson called by her office. He had a harried expression on his face and wasted no time in getting to the point.

'Jo, I need your latest computer print-outs. Will you get them organised for me?'

'Now?'

'Yes. Hunter wants to check over what we've accomplished so far. I'm to be up in his office at two o'clock with a complete rundown.'

'It's short notice. Did he say why?' she asked cautiously, a sick feeling invading her heart. She vividly remembered Mike's parting shot about her work.

'No, but it's within his rights to demand it at any time, so we jump,' he added wryly.

'I'll bring them around to you in ten minutes.'

'Thanks.'

Jo felt unaccountably nervous as she organised the data for Bob. There was nothing to be worried about. Whatever suspicions Mike might have concerning her integrity were completely unfounded; her work would soon testify to that. She quickly wrote an explanatory note on each print-out, placed them all in a folder and delivered it to Bob.

For two long hours she stewed over what was happening upstairs. Mike could be feeling vindictive. A man in his position could make life very difficult at the office. If he chose to put her work under a microscope as he had threatened, Jo was not sure she could cope with it. Her defences were brittle enough without having the confidence in her ability undermined. At last Bob returned, flopping down into her office chair and wiping his forehead in a telling gesture.

'Was he satisfied?' Jo asked impatiently.

'Yes—finally. He's certainly not in the best of moods today. Very tense and abrupt.' Bob took off his gold-rimmed spectacles and began wiping them in a slow, deliberate action. He suddenly shot her a sharp glance. 'You wouldn't know why, would you, Jo?'

She had no time to veil her reaction. She hoped her tension had not been too obvious. 'Elsie told me there'd been some trouble with his secretary. He fired her this morning,' she answered casually.

Bob shook his head and replaced his spectacles. He slouched further down in the chair, apparently intent on staying for some time. 'No,' he said consideringly, 'I don't think that was it. He was very particular about your results, Jo. It was a very pointed check on everything you'd done. Any reason for that?'

She shrugged. 'Maybe it's because I'm a woman.'

'Uh-uh—not that old chestnut, Jo! Hunter's not the type. I think you'd better tell me what's going on.'

'I don't know what you're referring to,' she answered tersely. 'You know perfectly well that the programme results are spot on. He has nothing to complain about.'

'No, you're quite right. And by now he knows that too. But I didn't like having to defend your work, and that's exactly what I've just done. If this contract is in some kind of jeopardy because of something personal between you, I want to know. I don't fancy being caught in the crossfire.'

Jo recognised that Bob was entitled to some explanation, but she found it quite impossible to discuss her involvement with Michael Hunter. 'The contract is not in jeopardy. He can't fault my work,' she repeated stubbornly.

Bob sighed and shifted uncomfortably. 'Look, Jo, I remember our first day here very well. Now, I have a strong feeling that I let you gloss over something that went pretty deep, something that generated enormous tension. Up until today I had no reason to pursue it further. It wasn't my business, and so long as you kept things on an even keel, that was fine by me. I found the office gossip rather reassuring.'

'What office gossip?' she snapped.

'Oh, come on,' he cut back irritably. 'This is no time for coy disclaimers. There's something between you and Michael Hunter and now it's causing a problem and the problem is involving me, so out with it, Jo. This isn't idle curiosity, this is business, and I need to be prepared for every eventuality.'

'I can't help what he thinks,' she blurted out defensively.

Bob remained unmoved, his expression demanding more information. Resentment washed hot colour into her cheeks and her eyes flashed defiance.

'I assured him on my first day here that I wouldn't let anything interfere with my work, and it hasn't,' she added bitterly. 'He can't say it has. If anything I've been more particular than usual. There's no problem. It's only in his mind.'

'What's in his mind?' Bob insisted quietly.

Jo looked away, hating each word that had to be spoken. Bob was not going to be pacified unless she gave him something concrete.

'The Hunters were involved in the death of my sister three years ago,' she stated baldly. 'It has nothing to do with the contract as far as I'm concerned.'

'But he's not quite sure,' Bob murmured, almost to himself. His hand began patting down his wispy hair, a sure sign that he was disturbed. 'One question,' he said ponderously. 'Did either of you expect to meet the other on that first day?'

'No. It came as a shock to both of us.'

'And Mark?'

'I knew of him. He'd never met me.'

'I see.' He nodded a few times, then muttered, 'A most unfortunate situation.'

Jo leaned forward, resting her elbows on her desk so that she could hold her head in her hands. She felt so tired, completely drained. 'I'm sorry, Bob. I probably should have asked to be replaced. I thought I could handle it, but now I'm not so sure. If he thinks. . . .'

'I made damned sure that he can't think anything but you're the best programmer he could buy, so you can stop worrying on that score,' Bob said dogmatically. 'In fact, I was rather abrupt myself, told him he was wasting his time and mine checking your work.'

'Thanks, Bob,' Jo murmured, grateful for his staunch support.

He sighed and pushed himself out of the chair. 'Pity about that office gossip—I thought you were well suited. Just shows how people can get the wrong end of the stick.' He gave her an encouraging smile. 'Cheer up now. Everything's on schedule and we're doing fine. That's all we've got to think about. And Jo,' he added softly, 'I'm sorry about your sister.'

She nodded, too choked up to speak. His sympathy weakened the last strand on her control and tears welled up in her eyes. Bob discreetly withdrew, leaving her to master her emotions in privacy. Jo wanted nothing else but to lay her head down and howl, but she stifled any sobs, swallowing them down in shuddering silence. Her hands kept her eyelids pressed shut, blocking off the threatening flood of tears.

Mike need not have made his intention so obvious to Bob. The emphasis was deliberate. He had wanted her to know, and Bob to know, that her work would be under scrutiny. The demonstration was designed to put them both on their mettle. It was her own fault for letting him believe the revenge motive. She should have corrected him, but it had not seemed to matter in the heat of the moment. She hoped the repercussions would not get any worse.

Each day blurred into the next. Jo kept telling herself that time would dull the heartache which stubbornly refused to be quelled. The days were not so difficult. She kept herself busy organising more work, driving herself and the other programmers to greater efforts. The nights were a torment. Her subconscious betrayed her then, taunting her with unfulfilled dreams. The lack of restful sleep and the intensity with which she worked gradually sapped her vitality.

It was on Thursday morning that her office telephone buzzed, demanding her attention.

'Jo Standish,' she answered promptly.

'Miss Standish, this is Linda Donnison, Mr Hunter's secretary. Mr Hunter would like to see you as soon as it's convenient. Would you give me a time, please?'

Jo's heart stopped dead and then began pounding erratically. 'Why? I mean, did he state a reason? Some business he wishes to discuss?' she explained hurriedly, covering her agitation with words.

'No, Miss Standish. My instructions were to make an appointment,' the girl answered carefully, obviously nervous of making a mistake.

Jo tried to think. She could not walk up there blindly, not knowing what he wanted. 'May I speak to Mr Hunter, please?' she asked decisively.

'Just one moment, Miss Standish, I'll see if I can get him.'

There was a long pause. Jo's mind raced over the possibilities, confused and anxious over the unexpected summons. At last Mike's voice came over the line, strong and deep.

'Yes, Jo?'

'Your secretary was not very explicit, Mr Hunter,' she began, stiffly formal. 'Do you want to see this week's results?'

She thought he sighed. His voice sounded tired when he spoke. 'No. Your work is no longer in any question, Jo. I would like to talk to you.'

Jo almost felt dizzy with weakness. 'What . . . what about?' she stammered. 'I mean, it is business, isn't it?'

There was a long pause. Then in an abrupt change of tone, his voice grated on her ear, harsh and cynical. 'Of course it's business, Jo. It couldn't very well be anything else, could it?'

'Mr Hunter, if you would kindly state what you require from me. . . .'

'I already have. I require your presence. By now you must be fully conversant with my programmers' capabilities. I want a definitive report on them. Am I asking too much to be given it today?'

The sardonic emphasis stung her to a quick retort. 'I'm free at the moment if that suits you.'

'Thank you.'

The swift disconnection was a reprimand in itself. Emotional turmoil raged inside her, making a mockery of all the careful defences she had built up during the week. Merely the sound of Mike's voice had brought them completely unstuck, and now she had to face him. In the short time it took to ride upstairs Jo managed a semblance of composure. There was no one occupying the reception desk, but Jo did not hesitate. Mike had said business and his secretary was probably with him.

'Come in,' he called in answer to her knock.

Jo took a deep breath and went in. Linda Donnison was not in evidence. 'Your secretary wasn't about, so I didn't know whether to wait or not,' she explained as hard blue eyes raked over her.

He stood up slowly and for the first time she found his strong physique intimidating. 'Please take a seat,' he invited in a deep monotone.

She moved forward quickly, relieved to take the chair indicated while Mike resettled himself behind his desk. When he remained silent she was forced to look up enquiringly. His expression told her nothing, his face a cold mask, the blue eyes guarded and watchful.

'I want to know if your good opinion of Neville McKay has been reinforced. Then give me a run-down of the others in order of competence and tell me if any of them should be replaced,' he demanded curtly.

Jo glanced down at her hands and consciously relaxed them. Her fingernails had been digging into the palms. There was no way she could control her pounding heart, but her brain was now functioning clearly. She proceeded to analyse each programmer according to his merits. She talked until there was no more to be said, and then the oppressive silence bore down on her.

'Thank you,' Mike said finally with very formal politeness. 'I'm pleased to hear that Barry Jensen has proved reasonably competent. I'll keep your recommendations in mind.'

'Is there anything else?' she asked, impatient to be gone now that the ordeal was over.

'Yes.' He pushed his chair back and stood up. 'There is one other question, Jo.' Very casually he strolled over to the coffee table, selected a cigarette from the onyx box and lit it. 'It appears that you don't carry your personal grudges into your work.'

'I told you that before.'

He gave a short, derisive laugh. 'You told me other things too, Jo, or have you forgotten? Your actions didn't quite measure up to your words.' He propped himself on the edge of his desk and looked down at her, eyes sharply probing. 'However, the question arises that if you're finished with your personal vendetta, why don't you look content? It's not every day one can pay off an old score so effectively. You should be pleased, glowing with satisfaction, instead of which you look pale and drawn, as if you haven't slept for a week. Now why should that be, Jo? You're beginning to worry people, people like our good friend Bob.'

Jo flashed a defiant look at him. 'I've been under a considerable strain this week, having been made aware of your suspicions regarding my work. Bob Anderson wasn't exactly delighted with his role on Monday.'

'I thought a check was justified under the circumstances,' Mike retorted wryly. 'However, I won't repeat the exercise. Anderson convinced me it was unnecessary.'

'Thank you,' she murmured, one heavy weight lifting off her heart. She lowered her head, unable to hold his gaze any longer. She watched her fingers absently pleating folds of material in her skirt. The business discussion was over and it was stupid of her to keep on sitting here, but somehow her feet were reluctant to make the move until Mike dismissed her.

'I told Bob he was mistaken,' he sighed suddenly. There was a momentary pause before he added sardonically, 'He had the quaint idea that you were crossed in love and that I was at fault. Naturally I corrected him, because that couldn't possibly be the case, could it? I mean, you've got what you wanted, haven't you, Jo? No regrets?'

He leaned back and stubbed out his cigarette in the ash-tray on his desk. Jo's lashes swept down to frustrate his probing eyes. She was too intent on hiding her vulnerability to even see him straighten and take the couple of steps that separated them. Suddenly he was looming over her and before she could utter a startled protest he had pulled her upright.

'Or has that fine line between love and hatred become blurred?' he suggested softly as he slid his arms around her.

'Don't! I'll scream if you touch me!' Jo cried out in frantic alarm.

'Scream, then, because I'm touching you, Jo.'

'Your secretary. . . .'

'Is not outside. Why are you trembling, Jo? Why aren't you stiff with outrage?' his voice taunted as his eyes burned down at her, reading the emotional chaos which was robbing her of resistance. 'Or do you want this as much as I do?'

It was as if she did not own her body any more. His hand caressed the nape of her neck and she just stood there mesmerised, knowing he was going to kiss her, letting him draw her closer. His hand moved slowly to tilt her chin upwards. She looked at his mouth, stared at it, surrendered to it even before his lips touched hers, softly, oh, so softly, sweet, seductive, drugging in its promise of love, and her need to be loved by this man drove everything else out of her mind, compelling her to respond. All the repressed passion burst free, hungry for satisfaction, demanding in its need to be fused with equal passion and exulting in the answer it received. Time had no meaning. The office they were in ceased to exist. Only she and Mike were real and they were one entity drowning in each other, sucked into a maelstrom of passionate need.

It was he who drew away, gentling her trembling body with all the tenderness of love. His breath was warm on her temples as he whispered to her, words full of choked emotion, urgent, pleading. 'You can't turn your back on this, Jo. Forget the past. My God, forget everything but what you feel at this moment! This is us, now, you and me, and you must know this is right.'

She could feel the throb of his heart, knew that her own marched with his, in step, in tune, rejoicing in unison, and she wanted this warm belonging to go on forever.

'Nothing is more important than this, Jo,' he murmured on, and she listened dreamily. 'We won't let anything intrude. Sailing—that's what we'll do. I'll take you sailing for the weekend, away from everything and everyone, and we'll just concentrate on each other and you'll see I'm right. We'll talk and make love and I'll make you happy. I swear it, Jo.'

Her heart cried out to accept. Give in—take what he was offering, it begged. She wanted to stay in the whirlpool, safely enclosed in Mike's arms. But the instinct for self-protection, the blind need for security, clawed its way uppermost. His arms weren't safe. One day they would drop her and then a chasm of desolation would open up and swallow her. To go with him would be against everything she had believed in.

'No!' She pushed herself away from him with a violence born of despair. 'I can't. You won't make me happy. I might be a weak fool, but I'm not that much of a fool. Let me go!' she almost sobbed as she stepped out of his reach, her chest heaving with the effort required to break free of him.

'Jo!'

The primitive need in his eyes stirred a response that terrified her. 'No!' she cried frantically. 'I won't be your woman. Don't ask me—I can't bear it!' Desperation was written on her face as she backed away. 'Leave me alone, Mike. Don't ask to see me again unless it's with Bob Anderson. You can trust my work—I promise you that.'

'I don't care about your goddamned work!'

She turned in sheer panic, but he caught her back against him before she could flee, his arms tight with possession.

'It's you I want, Jo—all I want. Don't run away from me. Give us a chance, Jo, please!'

She was panting. The struggle inside her was too intense. His hands cupped her breasts and the sexual pressure he was exerting jangled along her nerves. She stiffened. 'You said you didn't want my hatred, Mike, but you're earning it right now. Let me go!'

He swung her around so that she was forced to face him. 'I don't believe you. I don't believe you hate me—how can I, after that? Why are you doing this? A minute ago you were loving me.'

'No!' Jo denied wildly. 'Only my body, not my

mind. You're a good lover, you can arouse me. But it's not . . . it's not . . . oh, let me go! Find another Eva Daniels. I hate what you're doing to me. I won't be yours like that—not ever. Oh God, I do hate you!'

She twisted free from him, ran to the door and wrenched it open. She hurtled down the corridor and punched at the elevator button. The doors miraculously opened. Her feet stumbled in her haste and she pressed against the wall for support as the compartment whined downwards.

'I'm not going to think about it. I'm not going to think about it at all,' she repeated numbly. 'I was all right before I met Mike Hunter and I'll be fine if I keep him blocked out. That's all I have to do. It's stupid and destructive to love a man who only wants a mistress. I won't love him—I won't!'

By the time she returned to work Jo had achieved a protective mental fog. She did not attempt to concentrate on anything. Print-out sheets were spread on her desk, a pen was poised in her hand and occasionally she even turned a page, but nothing was done. At five o'clock she went home.

CHAPTER ELEVEN

THE weekend stretched ahead of her, and Jo felt panic welling up at the thought of all those empty hours. Somehow she had to fill them and ease the pressure on her heart and mind. On Friday night she did out all her kitchen cupboards, wiping them clean and re-organising the contents. She continued the process with her clothes closets until she was tired enough to sleep. On Saturday she went to a cinema complex in the city and sat through movie after movie. None of the plots made any coherent impression on her, but she watched them distractedly. The inactivity turned out to be a mistake, for she hardly slept at all that night.

On Sunday she determined to wear her body out with fatigue. She caught a bus to Ku-ring-gai Chase National Park. Her feet travelled over endless nature walks, following paths aimlessly until every muscle ached. By late afternoon she was satisfied that her purpose had been achieved. The trip back was tiresomely slow in the weekend traffic. It was almost dark when she finally walked the last few yards home. Her feet dragged up the stairs to her apartment. There was a clatter of footsteps behind her and she automatically glanced back over her shoulder. Mark Hunter was hurrying up the stairs below her.

'Hullo, Jo. I've been waiting for you to come home,' he said quickly as he caught her glance.

She gripped the banister tightly and turned to face

him, almost swaying with fatigue. 'What are you doing here? I thought you weren't coming back to Sydney for a while.'

'Mike sent for me on Friday—said he had to go away.'

'Oh!' Her heart gave a heavy lurch at the news. She mentally chided herself. Her reaction was absurd. The information that Mike was putting distance between them should have lightened her heart, not burdened it.

'I need to talk to you, Jo.'

'What for?' she blurted out. 'We have nothing to say to each other.'

'You might not have anything to say to me, but I certainly have a great deal to say to you,' he said in a decidedly grim tone.

Jo felt too tired to be polite. 'I don't feel like company, Mark, particularly not yours. I would have thought that had been made abundantly clear to you.'

'I'm not a complete fool,' he retorted with a touch of asperity, 'but this is important, Jo. I wouldn't have come if it wasn't, and I haven't waited around for almost three hours to be turned away now.'

'And just what is it that you consider so imporant, Mark?' she demanded, unwilling to let him into her apartment after her last experience with him.

'A man's life,' he answered curtly.

'What's that supposed to mean?'

'It means I'm going to straighten you out on a few facts. I don't feel sorry for you any more, Jo, not having seen what you've done to Mike. Now, are you going to let me come in, or do I have to say my piece out here on the stairs? I warn you you won't like it, but be damned if I'll go away without saying it. Take your pick. I'll shout it through the door if I have to.'

'Oh, come in then,' said Jo in a tone of exasperation. Although she told herself it was foolish, she was disturbed by the reference to Mike. 'Do you want a drink?' she asked tiredly.

'I wouldn't mind a Scotch if you have one.'

She poured out a generous measure and handed it to him before pouring out another for herself. 'Sit down,' she invited carelessly, waving towards the lounge. Having slipped off her sandals she curled up in an armchair and waited for him to speak.

He rolled the glass around in his hands as if he was warming brandy. 'It's time you faced up to the truth, Jo,' he opened bluntly.

'What truth?' she retorted, her tone dangerously brittle.

His eyes swept up to her with almost savage mockery. 'It may surprise you to know that I love Mike like a brother. I might occasionally scoff at him, put him down a bit, but I really depend on him, and he's always been my best friend.'

'Very commendable,' Jo muttered with weary sarcasm.

Mark ignored the comment. 'I can understand your attitude towards me. I don't think it's justified, but I can understand it.' He drew in a deep breath and his expression hardened to accusation. 'But what you did to Mike . . . that's something else again, and I'm not going to let it pass without. . . .'

'What I did to Mike!' Jo broke in with defensive scorn. 'My God, who do you think you Hunters are, expecting to take what you want when you want it, all on your own terms!'

'At least they're honest terms,' he flashed back angrily. 'By God! You'll hear the truth now if I have to ram it down your throat, and I don't give a damn if it hurts you. I've seen how much hurt you can dish out.'

'You dare to talk to me about hurting people!'

'Yes, I dare. I've just spent two days watching a strong man disintegrate, and you were the one who sledgehammered him, you with your sick idea of revenge for a past which you've got all twisted around.'

They glared at each other, resentments at boiling point. Jo took a defiant swig of whisky and Mark gritted his teeth.

'Right!' The word was grated out. 'We'll start with the night I met your sister.'

He paused, but Jo kept a baleful silence. After a quick swallow of whisky he began talking, eyeing her steadily like a prosecutor delivering his summation to the jury.

'I was in Sydney because Mike had gone off on a business trip. I was staying in his apartment and I felt depressed and lonely because Barbara had just refused to marry me. I'd been hitting the bottle too freely, and on sheer impulse I went up to King's Cross and settled myself at a table in the first Disco Club I sighted. I wasn't actually seeking company, I just wanted people and noise around me.

'I watched your sister dancing. She was quite an exhibitionist, a star performer, provocative, sexy and very pretty. Probably every man at the Club had his eye on her at one time or another. She attracted attention. I just sat there drinking. It was she who came to me, introduced herself and began chatting.

At first I wondered if she was on the game, picking me out as a possible client, but she told me she was a shop assistant in a dress boutique. She was quite amusing, and I didn't object to her company. Some hours passed and I let myself get too intoxicated. Carol suggested that maybe she should see me home, that I was in no condition to look after myself.

'And that's how it started. I woke up the next morning to find Carol in my bed, and let me tell you she was very obliging, and having been knocked back by Barbara, I didn't mind a pretty girl being obliging to me. Why not? She seemed to be a good-time girl, and I felt in need of a good time.'

'You're lying!' The accusation ripped off Jo's tongue. It was impossible to hold it back. The picture he was drawing was obscene.

'I'm telling the absolute truth,' Mark insisted harshly. 'Quite a number of people in Melbourne can vouch for it that I was besotted with Barbara at the time. I wasn't interested in any other woman. There was no way I'd set about seducing an eighteen-year-old virgin, not at any time, let alone just then. I was way down in the dumps and Carol handed me a tonic. I didn't ask her age, but I can tell you I was damned surprised when Mike said she was eighteen. I would have said early twenties, but even at eighteen she'd been around. Carol was no inexperienced virgin. If anything, she initiated our sexual relationship.'

'No!' Jo exploded vehemently. 'You're making out she was little better than a tramp. It's not true. Carol had too much pride in herself for that.'

His mouth curved sardonically. 'I agree. She was no common little tramp, ready to give herself to anyone. Carol had her eye too much on the main chance. She sized me up as a good bet, and one look inside Mike's apartment confirmed her calculation. You should have seen her drooling over his things —dollar signs were shining out of her eyes! And she got good value out of me. For three weeks I took her out wherever she wanted to go, dinner, shows, night-clubs. It filled in my empty hours and I didn't mind the expense. At her urging I even went shopping with her, bought her some gold ear-rings she admired, some Disco gear. . . .'

Jo stared at him, white-faced with shock. Some of the things he was detailing struck a sharp chord of memory. Carol had always been obsessed with clothes and jewelry, greedy for what she called the good things in life, luxury, high-class entertainment. She had also been very self-centred, expecting every-one to give in to her, and mostly everyone did. After all, she was pretty Carol, the personality girl, but Jo knew her sister's sweet cajolery had hidden a will of iron.

She had never imagined that Carol would use sex as a weapon too—sex appeal, yes, but not actually going to bed with a man, not in any calculating way. But if she thought it was the only way to get Mark and keep him. . . .

'Did you tell Carol that you were coming back to Sydney, that you'd see her again?' she asked ab-ruptly.

Mark made a grimace of impatience, as if Jo had missed the point entirely. 'Yes, I said I'd give her a call. I was expecting to return within the month, but Mike found he didn't need me after all.' His hands gestured an appeal. 'Look, Jo—it was just a casual way of saying goodbye. I probably would've given her a call if I'd come back, still unattached. As I said, we'd had a good time together, but she knew it wasn't serious. I'd even told her about Barbara.'

'But she would have thought you were finished with Barbara,' Jo muttered sadly, conceding at last that Carol could have had the determination to make her dream happen.

'Yes, I guess she would have thought that. I recall her saying that she'd mend my heart for me.' He sighed and bent his head, watching his hands rub together. 'Then came Mike's telephone call about Carol's pregnancy. I was furious with the fairy-tale you'd spun. It was so far from the truth it was laughable, only I wasn't laughing. I was marrying Barbara, and there was no way I wanted a pregnant Carol on my doorstep.'

He shot her a derisive look. 'What did you do, bewitch him? God, it made me even wilder when he wouldn't believe me. He kept on at me, trying to persuade me I could be wrong, that maybe I'd been too drunk that first night to know what I was doing with Carol, that she might have been an innocent. It was like an inquisition, begging Carol's case over and over and it was crazy, so far wrong it was ridiculous. Mike mentioned something about a sister and I told him I knew nothing of Carol's family. You were not spoken of once, Jo, I promise you.'

She nodded, believing him at last. Carol had not spoken of Mark, either, until she had needed help.

'When I finally argued him into believing me, I told Mike I'd pay up if he thought it was necessary,' Mark continued, 'but to make damned sure that Carol was really pregnant, because she'd told me all that was taken care of. All the talk of innocence made me think it was nothing but a con-job, and I said as much to Mike. I also made him promise not to give away my address because I was scared stiff how Barbara might react if Carol came down making trouble.'

Compassion softened his expression and brought a note of uncertainty to his voice. 'The next night Mike telephoned me and said that the matter had been resolved and there was no need for any financial arrangements. He sounded funny, very tired and strained, and when I started to ask him about it he just cut me off. I knew nothing about Carol's death or its circumstances until after Peg's party.'

Jo made no acknowledgement of his words. She had retreated inside herself, remembering Mike's cold, cold anger the night Carol died, remembering the contempt, the distaste on his face when Carol beat her fists into the cushions as she cried, 'But I love him, I want him. . . .' Oh yes, she understood now, understood the puzzlement in his eyes when Jo had flung the offer of money back in his face. Mike was a man who dealt in facts, and the facts had all been against Jo, if only she had known it. And afterwards, Carol's traumatic death had blinded her to everything else.

'That's the truth, Jo,' Mark was saying adamantly.

She heaved a sigh and looked at him with sad, empty eyes. 'Yes, I believe it is. Close enough to, anyway.'

He was startled, not expecting such a ready surrender from her. He hesitated, looking at her anxiously. 'Then surely you can see . . . Jo, your sister's death was an accident. You have no cause for revenge.'

'I don't want revenge,' she stated flatly. 'Oh, I admit I was tempted into bruising your ego a little, but I think we ended up about even on that, Mark.'

He shook his head in bewilderment. 'You're not making sense, Jo. You've done the cruellest damned thing you could do to a man. If it wasn't for revenge, what motive did you have for rejecting Mike so viciously?'

She stared down at her glass, idly fingering the rim as her mind struggled to resolve that question. She had been so wrong about Carol, and that hangover from the past had confused her relationship with Mike. For all her façade of self-sufficiency Jo knew that her deep inner loneliness cried out for the love and security of family which had been wrenched away from her three years ago. She had hated the Hunters because they had seemingly contributed to that loss, but with Mike she had begun to believe it could be replaced with another love.

She had desperately needed a love with no doubts at all, bound with the lasting security of marriage, but doubts had poisoned her trust in him and her intense vulnerability had made her react defensively. The dread of loving him and losing him had driven her to reject him. She could not bear that terrible pain of loss again.

'You must know that he loves you,' Mark said impatiently.

She glanced up, her eyes bleak with irony. 'Does he?' She sighed and stood up, turning her back on Mark and pacing away so that he could not see the pain she hugged to herself. 'You're mine for as long as I want you—that's what he said. *As long as I want you*. How do you think it feels to love a man who you know is going to put you out of his life when his appetite is satisfied? What kind of a love is that? I'd be swinging in the wind, waiting for the axe to fall, always watching for the signs of growing indifference. I couldn't bear it. I can't let him do that to me.'

She kept her back turned to him as tears streamed down her face. The emotion she had been stifling all week now threatened to swallow her up in one huge tidal wave. It was impossible to speak. There was a long fraught silence before Mark broke it.

'You've misunderstood him, Jo, just as he's misunderstood you. You really love Mike, don't you?'

She nodded, too distraught to care what he knew and reacting automatically to the soft sympathy in his voice.

'Why did you let him think you hated him?'

She moved over to the drinks cabinet and splashed some more Scotch into a glass, needing a fiery jolt to steady her chaotic nerves. She gulped some of it down and carried the drink back to her chair. 'It was the only way to make him let me go,' she answered dully.

'He does love you, Jo. He doesn't want a casual affair with you. It goes too deeply for that.'

Oh yes, she realised it now . . . too late. She had cut the tie between herself and Mike with brutal effectiveness. All her neurotic fears had blotted out the evidence of his love, but it was there all right, his determination to reach across the barriers, his caring for her when she was sick, his warm consideration and the love she had recognised in his eyes that night before . . . she closed her eyes, repressing the tears as she remembered his beautiful lovemaking . . . before she had killed it.

'What can I do?'

It was a cry of despair, but Mark did not recognise it as such. He breathed a sigh of relief and some of the strain left his face.

'Well, as I see it, you'll have to go to him, Jo. He won't come to you—not now. You've made it too hard.'

'I know,' she murmured.

'He won't be in any fit state tonight. He wouldn't like you seeing him the way he is. It had better be at the office in the morning.'

'Isn't he going away?'

'He has to pull himself together and brief me first. I'll see to that,' he said determinedly.

Jo hesitated and then blurted out, 'He won't see me. It's no use, Mark. It's worse than you know. He . . . I rejected him again on Friday morning.'

Mark stared at her. 'You mean, in spite of everything he tried again?'

Jo's cheeks burned with shame. She was already conscious of having dug her own grave without any emphasis from Mark.

'So that's why he telephoned me. All hope ground into dust. You really laid him out, didn't you, Jo?'

She shook her head in despair. 'It's just no use. He won't believe me. He'll think. . . .'

'Make him believe you,' Mark interrupted her forecefully. 'Mike will want to believe you, and God knows it's not difficult to show a man you love him if you really do. He's humbled his pride for you. Now it's your turn.'

She looked at him, her heart in her eyes, longing for release.

He drew in a sharp breath. 'My God! What have you two done to each other? I'll fix it,' he said decisively. 'I'll get Mike there and I'll have a private word to his secretary to let you into his office. Then it's up to you.'

'Thank you,' she whispered, intensely grateful for his interference and his help. It seemed strange that Mark, of all people, should be her ally in this.

Maybe the same thought occurred to him, for he leaned forward, resting his elbows on his knees and slanting her a wry look. 'Funny how life plays you up. I might have been happier married to Carol, she would still be alive, you and Mike wouldn't have got all twisted around.' He shook his head. 'And Barbara ran out on me anyway—no children, nothing. Was Carol really pregnant, Jo?' he asked gently.

'Yes. It was in the post-mortem. The police questioned me about it. There was a suggestion of suicide.'

'Oh, hell!' He wiped his hand across his face, then after a moment he shrugged off his depression and slowly climbed to his feet. 'I'd better get back to Mike. If he's come to, he'll probably be feeling pretty rotten.'

'Yes. Yes, of course,' Jo muttered, stirring herself to see him out. She touched his arm, embarrassed by having been so prejudiced against him and wanting to apologise. 'Mark, I've been a blind fool in too many ways to count, but I wish—at least, I hope you'll forgive me for being unkind to your feelings.'

'Hey, forget it!' he said softly. 'Think about tomorrow, not yesterday.' He gave her a cheering smile as he tilted her chin up with a finger. 'I want you two to be happy, so see that you make it work out. Okay?'

Tears shimmered in her eyes, but she managed a shaky, 'I'll try.'

'See you in the morning,' he nodded. 'Just after nine o'clock in Mike's office. Come straight on up and I'll make sure he sees you—alone.'

'Thank you.'

Jo watched him go, then slowly returned to her chair, too dazed by Mark's revelations to do anything but curl up and think about them. Mike really loved her. Maybe he had been going to propose marriage, but even if he did not want a legal commitment, he did love her, had loved her for years, and the love was deep and lasting.

She had panicked, lacking the courage to risk being hurt, lacking faith in a love which gave no guarantees. 'We belong together,' he had declared passionately, and Jo finally realised that 'for as long as I want you' had meant time continuing on and on. Mike held her future in his hands. She would never feel complete without him. Marriage or no marriage, she would go to him, be with him, give herself to him, but first she had to convince him of her love. That was not going to be easy, but she would do it. Somehow. Any way she could.

CHAPTER TWELVE

Jo rose early. She had slept surprisingly well, and the face which looked back at her from the mirror glowed with anticipation. Today was the most important day of her life, and she began it with intense preparation. Mike would not easily believe such a complete reversal of position on her part.

She groomed herself for him, overlooking no detail. All the disciplined concentration she had applied in trying to shut him out of her life she now unleashed on trying to win him back, completely singleminded in her purpose. She washed her long hair and blow-dried it to curl softly over her shoulders. No chignon today. She could not afford dignity or pride. Her eyes were accentuated with every make-up skill at her command. They were the one feature Mike had commented on, and she needed every advantage.

The dress she chose to wear had a sensuality which was not at all businesslike. The leopard-print flattered Jo's colouring and the silk jersey shimmered enticingly. The wrap-around style emphasised her curves and the loose bow at her waist drew the eye, suggestive of an easy removal. Mike had tried seductive persuasion on her last Friday. If words failed this morning, she was prepared to use the same tactics on him. She only had this one chance.

All the way to work her mind darted along different lines of approach, searching for the right words to convince him that she wanted whatever he wanted. Much would depend on how he reacted, but she geared herself mentally to bend those reactions her way. Failure was unthinkable.

'Wow!'

The long-drawn-out exclamation from Neville McKay summed up the other programmers' reactions when Jo arrived at the office. 'Good morning,' she muttered, and strode past them quickly, escaping to her own office before they recovered from their surprise at her appearance. It did not matter to her what they thought and she had no time for conversation. It was five minutes to nine. The next ten minutes dragged by while she fought to retain her positive thinking. A deep inner anxiety betrayed her as she picked up the telephone, her fingers fumbling as she dialled. Then Linda Donnison's voice came over the line, crisp and cheerful.

'Mr Hunter's office. Good morning.'

'Jo Standish speaking. Mark Hunter. . . .'

'Oh yes, Miss Standish. You're to come straight up.'

'Thank you.'

Jo stood up and straightened her dress. Mark had followed through on his promise. Now it was up to her. As she walked out all four programmers looked up curiously. She sailed past them without a word, heading straight for the elevators. The short ride up attacked her nerves. Despite all her will-power Jo's legs felt weak as she stepped out into the reception area. A slight girl was occupying Susan Trigg's desk. She looked neat and pleasant and her welcoming smile steadied Jo a little.

'Miss Standish?'

'Yes.'

'I'm Linda Donnison. Mr Mark Hunter is conferring with Mr Michael Hunter at the moment, but you're not to wait. Shall I take you in?' she asked, a little uncertainly.

'No, thank you. It's all right.'

Jo walked slowly down the short corridor, a tumult of emotion overtaking her on the way. She suddenly felt like a prisoner on the last walk to the gallows, with heaven or hell waiting inevitably behind Mike's door. For a moment she hesitated, then with set determination she knocked and went in without waiting for an answer.

Both men were bending over Mike's desk. Mark straightened more quickly, giving a slight, satisfied nod. Mike stared at her, his expression completely unreadable.

'May I speak to you, Mike?' she asked rather shakily.

He did not answer.

'Excuse me,' Mark muttered, attempting a swift exit.

'Don't go, Mark!' It was an order. 'I'm sure Jo would prefer you to remain here.'

'I'm afraid I can't oblige,' Mark replied, and promptly ignored the order, closing the door behind him with a firm hand.

Mike's gaze flicked back to her, a muscle contracting in his jaw as his eyes roved over her. 'You surprise me, Jo. What brings you to me, without Anderson at your side?'

She flushed at his pointed reference to last Friday's confrontation. 'What I have to say is a private matter.'

He hesitated, his eyes instantly wary. 'Very well.'
The words carried an air of resignation. He sat back
down at his desk and rubbed a hand across his face in
a gesture of immense weariness. When his gaze
returned to her it was all bleak formality. 'Won't you
sit down?'

'Thank you,' she murmured, not sure if she
wanted to sit or not. She was far too tense to relax,
but she took the chair he indicated.

He forestalled any words from her by taking the
initiative. 'I must apologise for taking such an unfair
advantage of my position last Friday. It was . . .
unethical, to say the least. It won't happen again. In
fact I'm leaving the office today and won't be back
until after your contract is completed. I'm sure you'll
carry it through competently. Mark will be taking
over here, but he won't make any personal demands
on you. Your position will be quite free of disturb-
ance from either of us. I'm only sorry that. . . .' He
paused and gave a light shrug. 'However . . . what
can I do for you? Or have I just removed the
necessity to speak at all?' he added with a wry twist of
his lips.

Jo took a deep breath and plunged straight to the
heart of the matter. 'I don't want you to go, Mike.
You had it right, last Friday. I do love you and I do
want us to be together like you said. I was crazy, all
mixed up, but if you'll give me another chance. . . .'

'Stop right there, Jo,' he interrupted curtly.

Her eyes begged him to listen, but he closed his
own against her pleading, pinching his eyelids between finger and thumb as if to squeeze out any
softening.

'It's no good—I can't take any more of your

love-hatred.' The words dragged out on a long sigh, and his eyes opened and swept over her with no spark of interest. They seemed withdrawn, empty of all emotion. 'I'm removing myself from any contact with you. I won't be tempted into that insanity again. The dream turned into a nightmare, but I'm awake now and I'll survive without you. You keep your shadow world, Jo. It's too dark with passions I don't understand, and what I don't understand I can't fight. There's no more to be said.'

Jo knew she had to jolt him, shake him out of his defensive armour. 'All I've done was to protect myself from you. You weren't the only one with a dream. I thought mine was coming true, but then you smashed it and it's taken me a while to adjust to something else. But I do love you and I don't want to lose you. I know that now. I'll be yours for as long as you want me,' she added haltingly.

The blood rushed up her neck in a hot flood. She thought how strange it was that it was difficult even now to say those words. Her eyes pleaded dumbly with him, large green pools of pain, contrasting sharply with the deep blush that stained her cheeks. At least she had succeeded in sparking some interest. His eyes were probing now and there was a quality of stillness about him that suggested sharp concentration.

He frowned, obviously puzzled by her assertions. 'You said you couldn't bear it. If it wasn't because of the past, why was my love so unacceptable to you? You rejected it, so. . . .'

'No!' she rushed in, not letting him remember the pain. 'I couldn't bear the kind of relationship you were offering me. I ran from you because I was frightened of accepting and I thought it would only lead to misery, but it's no use running. I won't ever feel this way for anyone else and at least I'll have you for a while, if you'll let me.'

'I don't want. . . .' He stopped, his voice gathering force. 'What in God's name did you think I was offering you?'

Tears blurred her eyes and she could not speak over the lump in her throat. Mike made an impatient sound and she shook her head, fighting to regain control. 'It doesn't matter,' she finally choked out.

He leaned forward and spoke with deep urgency. 'Jo, I've got to know. If you don't let me into your mind we'll never sort out the problems.'

'You said you wanted me,' she blurted out, panic creeping into her voice. 'I don't know what you intended—you didn't say. You kept saying you wanted me, that I should be yours. I thought you meant us to be lovers. You asked me to go sailing with you for the weekend. Talk and make love, you said.'

'And didn't you want the same?' he asked softly, calming her agitation.

She nodded.

'Then why the rejection?'

'I haven't . . . I've never . . .' She stared at him helplessly, imploring him to stop the questions, to just take her and love her.

'Go on,' he insisted quietly.

'I told you. I warned you I couldn't trust anyone, not after . . . not after what happened to Carol, and you—you let me down. I know now that I had it all wrong and I don't blame you for anything, but don't you see? Don't you remember how she was that night when she knew it was over and Mark didn't want her any more? I swore I'd never let any man do that to me. I swore I'd never give myself to anyone unless. . . .'

'Unless?'

She had gone too far, let herself get carried away. His face looked more haggard than before, the lines deeply etched. She had to get back on to the course she had set herself, giving, not demanding. She forced herself to stand and move.

'I don't care any more. I love you and I don't care what you ask of me.' Mike was standing too and she felt a nameless fear grip her heart. She held out her hands in a last, desperate appeal. 'I'll give you anything you want if you'll just love me. Please, Mike. . . .'

Her last words were muffled as he crushed her against him in a fiercely possessive embrace. She shuddered with relief, closed her eyes and savoured the warmth and strength of his body.

'Forgive me, my darling,' he murmured huskily, stroking her hair in soft comfort. 'I had to be sure. It's been such hell. If only I'd understood your fears!' He gently tilted her head back and a soft gaze of love gave her all the assurance in the world. 'Jo, I seem to have been waiting for you all my life, and the rest of my life would be barren without you. Will you be my wife?'

'Is that . . . is that what you really want, Mike? You're not just saying it?' she asked, hope quivering in her heart.

'I want whatever you want. Your happiness is mine. You're the only woman I've ever loved and to have your love means everything to me. Now, will you marry me?'

'Oh yes, Mike. Yes, yes, yes!' she answered fervently.

They smiled at each other, a joyous smile of complete understanding, and instinctively their mouths drew together and they kissed with hungry passion, yearning to be one in body as well as mind. For a long time they clung together, exulting in the wonderful pleasure of knowing this was only a beginning.

'How could you think I would ever have enough of you?' he breathed as he moved his lips in a reverent trail around her face. 'I'm only half alive without you.'

'Oh, Mike, I feel the same way,' she whispered. 'I've been an awful fool, not trusting you.'

He placed a silencing finger on her lips and looked down at her with a tenderness that squeezed her heart.

'I love you. I love everything about you, and the past is as nothing, because the future is really ours, and just now I feel happier than I thought was humanly possible.'

He kissed her again to prove it, and the kiss stirred another fiery outpouring of need answering need. They did not hear the door rattle open behind them.

'Coffee, Mr Michael? Oh—er—pardon me!'

'Don't go, Elsie,' Mike called after her rapidly retreating figure. He gave Jo a teasing smile and murmured, 'Maybe we need some coffee to sober us up.'

'Don't let me interrupt nothin',' Elsie retorted, well satisfied with what she had seen.

They laughed after her swiftly departing figure, too happy to care what anyone thought.

'She can't wait to get to let everyone know,' Mike declared, then suddenly sobered. 'And speaking of that subject, a visit to Melbourne this weekend will definitely be expected once I tell my parents. In fact, my mother won't be able to wait to welcome you with open arms. She'd given up hope of my ever marrying. Will you come?'

'I'd love to, Mike. I'd love to meet all your family.'

'You undoubtedly will,' he grinned. 'But I'm warning you now—they'll all swoop in like vultures to pick you over.'

'I don't mind,' she laughed. 'At least you have a family.'

He gently squeezed her hand and his eyes promised her everything. 'We'll have a family of our own as soon as you want, Jo. You'll never be alone again.'

'I love you, Mike Hunter,' she whispered fervently.

'You can keep telling me that for the rest of our lives and it will never lose its wonder for me. I didn't really believe my dream, and yet you've given it to me. I'll try not to fail you again, Jo.'

'You didn't fail me, Mike.'

'That's your forgiving heart speaking,' he smiled, but there was humility in his eyes. 'I failed you all along, always expecting less than you really were. My cynicism kept leading me astray, first on that night your sister died and then when we met again. At Peg's party I looked at you and you were so very beautiful. I suddenly saw how desirable you were to other men besides myself. Much as I hated the thought, I couldn't believe you hadn't had any lovers. After all, I'd been with other women and I had no right to expect you to be any different. All that really mattered was that you were mine in the end.

'I never envisaged an affair with you, Jo. It was always marriage that I wanted, you at my side in a lifelong love affair. I didn't want to pressure you, so I said nothing, waiting for you to work out your own feelings, but when you told me that you loved me, I couldn't control what I felt. The long wait was finally over and I wanted you so much, to hold you in my arms and know it was really true. I didn't think of giving you reassurance—I thought you knew it was so special it had to last for ever.' He sighed and there was a deep apology in his eyes. 'I must have said all the wrong words to make you turn against me. There were so many words bottled up in me I don't know what came pouring out.'

'It wasn't only the words, Mike. I was a little frightened anyway, because it was new, and although it felt right, I also felt as if I was being rushed along. Instead of love and marriage, you spoke of want and possession, and I began to panic. Then I remembered Carol and all the old nightmare rushed in on me, and suddenly you were the Michael Hunter I couldn't trust. It was like being torn in two. I'm sorry, Mike—I couldn't help myself.'

He raised her hand and kissed it before lovingly holding the palm against his cheek. 'And I swore I'd never hurt you again. Always tell me what's on your mind, Jo. Don't hold back. I don't want any more misunderstandings between us—we've wasted too much time already.'

'Then you must promise not to make it hard for

me,' she smiled. 'When you sat there behind your desk you looked totally unreachable. I'd deliberately dressed up to seduce you if necessary, and then you looked at me so coldly I almost froze inside.'

He laughed. With the torment safely past it was possible to laugh. 'I put that desk between us because you were so beautifully desirable I couldn't trust myself. I don't know how I looked, but it was almost an intolerable strain to retain control. There was a volcano inside me, but once I realised you meant what you said, Jo, I had to draw you out. I couldn't risk losing you again.'

Her eyes danced at him. 'What! A tenacious man like you, Mike Hunter? Admit the truth now—you were determined to wear me down to total surrender.'

He grinned at her. 'I love you so much, nothing else would do—and you're right, I am a tenacious man.' He kissed the third finger of her left hand. 'What I have, I'll hold.'

It was a promise, giving Jo all the security she had ever craved, and her eyes thanked him, glowing with the love he had sought and won.

Harlequin Plus

THE REAL CASANOVA

"He's a real Casanova!" How many times have you heard this description applied to men who trifle with women's affections? Men known for a succession of love affairs that have ended in heartbreak? Let's take a look at the honest-to-goodness real thing—the original Casanova, the man who made the pursuit of women—and other pleasures—a way of life.

The son of an actor, Giovanni Casanova was born in Venice in 1725. In a sense Casanova followed in his father's footsteps, for during his colorful lifetime he played many roles. After being expelled from a seminary for immoral behavior, Casanova pursued careers as violinist, gambler, diplomat, and spy. He was forever fleeing some country or another after a scandal involving a woman—usually the wife of another man—and once even made a spectacular escape from a Venetian prison.

As rakish as his manner of living may seem today, Casanova's life-style was considered ideal by the gentlemen of the time; the aristocracy of Europe's capitals was devoted to the pursuit of pleasure, with very little thought given to the consequences.

But during his lifetime—which seemed overflowing with incredible escapades and illicit romantic liaisons—Casanova somehow found the time to write. One of his most famous works is entitled *Story of My Life,* a vivid, though doubtless somewhat exaggerated—we think!—account of his many amorous adventures.